THE CHOICE BETWEEN US

Edyth Bulbring

First published in 2019 by Tafelberg, an imprint of NB Publishers
This edition published by Edyth Bulbring, 2020

ISBN: 978-1-990941-31-3

For Mike

MARGARET

24 Pembroke Street,
Sydenham,
Johannesburg.
17 May 1963

My name is Margaret Beatrice Channing-Court and I am nine years old. I would like to be your pen pal. My hobbies are reading and collecting stamps, and I am a Brownie. I am trying for my sewing badge next week. Hold thumbs.

My finger rests on the page as I stop writing. "I can smell you, Benny Scumbucket. Don't even *think* about creeping up on me." I sit back, flip the page over, and twist the cap of the fountain pen. I wait for him to show himself.

Benny breaks the silence. He breathes out through his nose, making a whistling noise. "Ag, no man, Mags. How do you always do that? I don't stink. And you must stop calling me Scumbucket."

I turn around and give him my bored face, making one

1

eye squiff. Benny crouches on his knees behind my chair, ready to pounce. He's all red in the face and his lip lifts in a snarl. My mother says Benny's got a harelip and it's rude to stare. I'm used to it now and most times I hardly notice.

I don't call him Hairy-lip or Fang. I also never say: "Eat with your mouth closed." Or, "If you make that ugly face the wind will change and you'll stay like that for ever. Ag, shame, too late, hey?"

Other children say things like this to him all the time and think it's funny. I just call him Scumbucket. He whines about it but I know he secretly likes it.

"What you doing?" He gets up off the floor and wanders around the room, fiddling with the things on the shelves. He can never keep still, always fidgeting.

"None of your beeswax." I'm not going to tell Benny about my new pen pal hobby. If he knew, he'd copy me and beat my stamp collection. I've already written seven letters. Fingers crossed, in a few weeks' time, I'll be getting replies from places like Sweden, Australia and England.

I'll use the kettle to steam the stamps off the envelopes, and then stick them in my album. Benny uses special sticky tape because he says glue damages the stamps and I won't be able to sell mine one day. I don't care, I've got more stamps than him.

"Out of your daddy's study. Out of here."

The annoying voice belongs to Gemima. My mother says everyone has a cross to bear. The cross my mother bears is her poor health, mine is Gemima. She's my nanny and I've known her since the day I was born at the Marymount Hospital nine years and three months ago. I came early. Gemima says I couldn't wait to get out into the world and start causing trouble.

I spent the first couple of years of my life strapped tight to Gemima's back with an old towel my mother gave her because it was too shabby for our bathrooms. As soon as Gemima put me down, I'd start crying and she couldn't get the housework done. For twenty-four months, my face was squashed against her. Awake, I stared up at her doek.

I didn't start walking until I was two, and never learnt to crawl. I just pulled myself across the floor on my bottom. My father says children who don't crawl have learning difficulties at school. I'm terrible at sums. I blame Gemima.

The first word I said was "Mima". I wish I hadn't because it made Gemima as pleased as punch. She was forever telling the other nannies this story. But she told my mother my first word was Mama, which sounds like Mima.

If she'd told my mother the truth, it might have hurt her feelings. Mothers can be so sensitive. Mine spends a lot of time in her bedroom with the curtains closed because she suffers from ghastly headaches. When she feels better, she sews like a maniac until her head explodes. I've got clothes for Africa.

"Come on, outside with you! Your daddy will be home soon."

Gemima shoos us out of the study, her fingers flapping at the back of our legs. She shuts the door behind us. "Supper will be ready just now, so don't you dare go near that loquat tree."

Benny and I go out into the garden and head straight for the tree. We stuff our faces until we each have a fistful of pips. I make sure we've got the same amount. Benny wants to go first, but it has to be fair.

With a tap on my chest, I begin: "Eeny, meeny, miny, moe, catch a ..."

Benny grabs my finger. "Stop. My mom doesn't like it when you say that word." He bends my finger back. "Anyway, you know when you start with yourself I'm always out. So just go, okay?"

We stand apart and take turns, three goes each, spitting pips at each other. Every time I score a hit, I take one step forward. When I miss, I take one step back.

The sky is red. Red in the night is a sailor's delight. Red in the morning, a sailor's warning. Johannesburg is a million miles from the sea so we don't have sailors, just mine dumps. In a few minutes, the orange sun will slip down behind the koppie and the street lights will flicker on.

By five o' clock, some of the nannies are on their way home to the location. Not Gemima. She stays in the room outside our house in the back garden just to torment me, I know. Even though she says her home is too far away. It's on my Uncle Frank's farm in Natal.

"Fine, you win," says Benny. "What do you want to play next?" He tosses his pips on the ground and spits one out of the side of his mouth.

It's my turn to decide. Yesterday it was Benny's. We played hide and seek. I went first, and hid above the cupboard in my bedroom. I fell asleep and only woke up when Gemima came to put the washing away. She said Benny went home and swore he wouldn't play with me any more. He's forever saying he'll never, ever, *ever* play with me again – but then who else would play with him?

I pretend to think, but I already know what I want to play. "Tok-tokkie. You can go first."

I make a smile as sweet as golden syrup. Benny's a cowardy custard and he never wants to go first.

His face flushes and he kicks a pine cone across the lawn through the spray of the sprinkler. "I'm not allowed. If I get caught again my mom's going to punish me."

Mrs Schaumbacher doesn't believe in beatings or sending children to bed without supper. When she punishes Benny, he isn't allowed to read his comics or listen to his programmes on Springbok Radio. I'd take the sjambok any day.

Benny's father goes away a lot, for months sometimes, so Benny's mother says she has to be two parents in one. She's being a dad when she punishes Benny. If she's not strict with him he'll go to the dogs. When she comforts him at night because he's scared of the bogeyman, she's being a mom. It must be jolly confusing trying to be two parents.

"We won't get caught. Come on, man, don't be a drip."

Benny nods. "But nickies not on."

"Scaredy-cat, catch a rat. Put it in your Sunday hat."

His face twists. Sometimes he gets so cross with me he just

goes home. It's no fun playing tok-tokkie on my own.

"Fine, I'll go first." I give him a smile full of teeth to make him nice again.

Gemima comes across the lawn towards us, dodging the sprinkler. She's tied her doek neatly, and she's wearing a clean apron over her pink uniform. "I'm just going over the road to Sophie, I'll be back now-now. You two play nicely here." She tucks her church sewing bag under her arm and walks a few steps. She turns and wags her finger at me. "Quietly, hey. Your mummy's head is worse today."

Sophie is also a nanny, and she's got a room at the back of the house across the road. They belong to the same church. Methodical Methodists, that's what my father calls them. Gemima goes to church every Sunday after clearing away the breakfast plates. She wears a badge on the pocket of her red-and-black church uniform. It says *IOTT*, and Gemima told me this means I only take tea. I know she drinks coffee too, so it's not quite true, but what the Methodists don't know can't hurt them.

We wait until she is out of sight. All clear. Benny and I wander into the street and cross the road to the house next door to where Sophie stays. I sprint through the gate up to the front door, keeping close to the edge of the path next to the bushes. I grab the brass knocker and slam it down five times and run back down to where Benny's hiding behind a lemon tree. He's laughing like a drain.

We crouch down, staring at the front door. I hold my breath. "Shoosh, stop it, man." I smother his mouth with my hand. I feel the scar above his lip. I don't mind touching it.

The front door opens and Mr Dickson peers around. He takes a few steps down the path and then turns back and slams the door. We wait. And wait. Come on, Mr Dickson, come on! Some days he doesn't behave the way we want him to. It's getting boring.

"Your turn." I nudge Benny.

My knees pop as we stand up and walk away from the house. The sun has dipped, the sky is purple. Benny is a dark shape before me on the path.

"Blerrie terrorists. I'm going to blow your heads off," says a voice.

"Chips! He's coming. Run, for your life, Benny. Run!"

We run. I'm laughing so much I can't breathe. Benny is snorting. I look back. Mr Dickson's got his shotgun and he's wobbling down the path. The gun goes off behind us and we dodge through the gate.

"I'll get you. Blerrie baboons."

We duck next door through the service entrance and race towards the back, to the washing line and rubbish bins. The door to the outside room is open. I dive inside.

"Hide us, hide us. Mr Dickson's got a gun and he wants to kill us." Mr Dickson only fires blanks. But I'm holding thumbs that one day he'll use live ammo.

Sophie is sitting on the narrow iron bed and Gemima is on the floor, her legs stretched out on a piece of cardboard, fingers busy with her embroidery. I crawl under the bed while Benny squeezes behind the door. We wait. Sometimes Mr

Dickson comes looking for us. Maybe today is one of those lucky days.

Sophie's bed is raised off the floor. Three bricks under each leg. My mother says the natives like to sleep high off the ground so the tokoloshe can't get them. They're scared of the tokoloshe because they are superstitious and ignorant. I think Sophie's right to be safe rather than sorry. Everyone knows tokoloshes eat your brains when you're sleeping.

I peek through Sophie's dangling legs. Her heels are cracked, her soles yellow with knobbly corns. I spot dust bunnies, and a stray hairclip in a corner of the room.

A square of yellowed newspaper covers a pane in the window. It's high up on the opposite wall, allowing only a teeny bit of light into the room. Sophie doesn't have a cupboard. Her blue shweshwe dress and her pink uniform are hanging from nails on the wall.

The room is a lot smaller than Gemima's, and I can't see any photographs. Gemima has a framed snap of my father and her when they were children on the farm in Natal. It sits on the crate by her bed, next to a jam jar with everlasting flowers. My father has the exact same photo in his study. But Sophie doesn't have a desk or a crate, and she decorates her walls with pictures of smiling ladies from *Drum* magazine, which Gemima also reads.

We wait for ages. I peep at Gemima. She stares at me, her nostrils quivering. Her dark eyes tell me she's going to get me as soon as we're back home.

I hold her stare, my lips moving silently: *Stare, stare, like a bear. Sitting on a monkey's chair. When you lose your underwear. That will teach you not to stare.* I pretend to lick my lips but Gemima and I both know I'm sticking my tongue out at her.

I hear the sound of breathing behind me. Skrikked, I look back. Not a tokoloshe. It's an African. She's curled up, pressed against the wall, trying to make herself small. The doek is skew on her head and her uniform is grubby. Her eyes are big and white in a black face, shiny with sweat. She touches her finger to her lips and we stare at each other until she closes her eyes. Her lashes flutter

"You can come out now, Margaret," Gemima says.

I look back at the nanny and touch my finger to my lips before scrambling out from under the bed.

On our way home, Gemima grips Benny and me by the hands as we wait to cross the road. I try to wriggle away. I'm not a baby. I know how to cross the road. But she clutches my hand tighter. We look left, then right. As we look left again, a police van squeals around the corner and comes to a stop as its front wheel hits the side of the pavement.

Two policemen jump out, and one of them sprints towards a group of Africans walking towards the bus stop. He waves a short black stick at them and yells. They run, screaming fit to raise the dead.

The police are always chasing the Africans when they leave work to travel home to the location, or go off for their half-day on Thursdays. The nannies run and try to hide in the back rooms, but the police often catch them. If they find the

African under Sophie's bed there'll be hell to pay.

The other policeman comes up to us, and he looks like he means business. Next to me, Benny makes a sudden move, his mouth hanging open wider than usual, as if he's going to cry.

"It's all right," I say to him. "Really, it's fine. We can't be in trouble." I smile but my voice cracks. Surely Mr Dickson wouldn't have set the police on us. That's never been part of the game.

Gemima lets go our hands and stares down at the ground as the policeman reaches us.

He stops in front of her. "Dompas." He holds out a hand. The fingernails are black with dirt.

She reaches into her apron pocket and offers him a small dark-coloured book. He flips through the pages, drops it on the ground, turns to leave. As he walks off, Benny throws up at my feet. A yellowy-orange, sticky loquat mess.

I shift away, my takkies are splattered. "Sis, man, Benny."

"Sorry." Benny kneels on the ground, looking up at me, his chest still heaving. I glare at him and the mess at my feet. Gemima's going to be mad that we stuffed ourselves before supper. I hand him my handkerchief to clean up.

We watch as the policeman shoves three Africans into the back of the van. He yells as he pushes. "I don't care if you left your donderse pass books at home. You kaffirs must learn to wear them around your neck." He slams the door shut and bangs on the metal grille.

Benny goes home and Gemima drags me into the kitchen.

The pressure cooker is shooting steam all over the room. She reaches into a drawer and pulls out the wooden spoon. It has a name: Gemmy. This makes it sound friendly. But it's not.

She always catches me if I try to run away, so I just show her the palms of my hands and sigh. Benny's nanny isn't allowed to smack him. But my father says Gemima's mummy also had a wooden spoon on the farm and it never did him any harm.

I stare at Gemima with my hating eyes as she slams the spoon down. I don't pull my hands away. She hits harder than usual, her face tight.

"*That's* for not listening to me. *That's* for playing your stupid game and teasing that poor old man. *That's* for the loquats. And *that's* to remind you to be good tomorrow."

To get her back I'm going to wish the tokoloshe on her. It will eat her brains tonight when she's asleep. I cross fingers on both my hands and make the wish as she tells me to sit down.

Gemima butters a slice of white bread, sprinkles sugar on top, and puts it on a plate in front of me. I keep my hands in my lap away from the bread until her back is turned.

I hear my father at the front door. He is putting his doctor bag next to the telephone table, his hat and jacket on the hook in the hallway next to my school blazer. He comes through to the kitchen, strokes the top of my head, and greets Gemima.

"Everything all right, Ntombi?" My father has always called her this, ever since they were children on the farm. It's Zulu for girl. "How were things at home today?" He relies on her to give him a rundown of the day's events. Whether my mother ate lunch, or left the bedroom to sit and sew. And whether I behaved.

"Was Margaret a good girl?"

I rub my red palms together. I know she's going to tell on me.

Gemima smiles, her eyes steely as she glances down at me. "She was as good as gold, Doctor C-C." Everyone calls him this. Channing-Court is a mouthful and a half.

She doesn't tell my father about Mr Dickson and the gun. And I don't tell him about the African I saw hiding from the police under Sophie's bed. It's our secret.

Some days, Gemima and I understand each other. Perfectly.

JENNA

Dear Teen Agony Aunt
I want to divorce my mother. Please advise me
how to do this. ASAP.

Yours sincerely
Miserable At Home (15 years old)

Yes, I wrote this email. In February, a whole month ago. I'm still waiting for a response but I guess Aunty Agony thought I was trying to be funny and deleted it. Except, I wasn't joking. See, my name is Jenna Moore but I'm also Miserable At Home.

I use the "home" word loosely. It's just a house where I live with my mom until my dad discovers my existence and rescues me from domestic hell.

The idea of divorcing my mother didn't come from nowhere. I read about a sixteen-year-old girl who actually tried it. In her case the dad was the problem. He was too strict on her. My mom doesn't care what time I go to bed, if I do my homework, what my report says, or if I bunk school. She isn't an uptight dictator, she's just totally hopeless.

It's dark outside, and I'm in bed listening to the rain

13

thudding on the roof. Trickling down my bedroom wall. The cooking pot propped against my feet, catching the water dripping from the ceiling, is close to overflowing. Plop. Plop. Plop. I'm not kidding. The roof's a colander.

My mother tiptoes into my bedroom and swops the pot with a bucket, trying to make as little noise as possible. She's not big on confrontation and believes in letting dogs and hormonally challenged teenagers sleep.

"I thought you got the roof fixed?" My voice – soft, but hard – stops her at the doorway. Busted!

Our roof has been fixed more times than I've had sex. Not that I've had any, so it's not such a hard number to beat. My mom collects hot handymen like spare change. The first "builder" was Useless Trevor, then Useless Graham and after them guys whose names I can't remember. They all said that the roof was as tightly sealed as a priest's lips after confession. They took our cash and ran, leaving us to deal with the leaks.

"Maybe I can track Phineas down. He was cute. But he must have overlooked a couple of things." My mother shrugs, wrinkles her nose in a way some men find appealing. Yes, Useless Phineas, that's him. He was the last one *not* to fix the roof.

"What an awesome storm!" She laughs as lightning cracks and rain slams down on our tin roof.

Yes, awesome.

If you met my mother you'd probably think she was cool. "Call me Holly. Mrs Moore is too old. Jenna calls me Holly too, don't you, baby?" I do. Always have. Calling her Mom would be like Cinderella's sister trying to squeeze her fat foot into the glass slipper. It could never, ever fit.

"I'm too young to lay all that mumsy crap on you, that's for other people. We're different, I want us to be besties." She pulls me close and squeezes the breath out of me as she says this.

Like, really? Why would a fifteen-year-old girl want to be best friends with a thirty-three-year-old woman?

If your dad met Holly and me he'd look us both up and down and his eyes would settle on her. Maybe for a bit too long. On the belly ring peeping out from under her T-shirt or the daisy tat on her left shoulder. He'd probably say something like: "So, which one of you is the older sister?" It's sickening.

I can't introduce you to my dad because he isn't around. Hasn't been for the past fifteen years. A bit scarce, really, like world peace.

Holly got "knocked up" during her first year at university. Whoopsie! As if someone just knocked against her and she fell. Up rather than down.

Wingardium Leviosa! And there I was, her little floating bun, fresh out of the oven.

Holly was open with me about it right from the get-go. Some mothers don't play it straight with their kids. Let's face it, there's a two-thousand-year religion, courtesy of a mother who didn't 'fess up. No, Holly's a fierce believer that honesty is the best policy even when it guts your four-year-old kid, and actually, a few white lies would have done the trick in the meantime.

"Sorry, baby, your dad and I just didn't work out and he wasn't too keen on a kid. He ran for the hills. But you've got *me*, haven't you?"

Class act.

"He was a really nice guy, just commitment phobic. Maybe next year I'll make contact and the two of you can meet up. Now's not a good time."

It was never a good time.

Holly fishes in my laundry basket and pulls out a red-and-white checked dress, giving it a couple of vicious swipes to straighten out the creases. "I'll get to the washing later on. But this one's fine for school today, isn't it?"

"Please, just get out of my room and leave me alone."

I'm still pissed off at Holly. It was about a month ago that we had the most brutal conversation of my life (fight, actually). I don't know if Holly and I can ever go back to being normal again. In our case, abnormal.

I found out something she'd kind of forgotten to tell me. For Holly, this isn't lying. But it wasn't the sorry-I-used-the-last-of-the-milk-in-my-coffee forgetfulness.

I'd been on at Holly about my father. Was he tall, like me? Did he also hate cauliflower? When can we meet? And then she lost it with me. I guess she was hung over.

"Enough already, Jenna. Give it up, won't you? He doesn't even know you exist, okay?"

Boom! Her words were a hand grenade in my face.

"You never told him about me?"

Holly turned away and filled a glass of water at the sink.

She gulped it down, dribbling at her chin. "I'm sorry, baby, I really am. Please, just let it go."

Let it go. Give it up. Like deleting spam clogging up my inbox.

I got up and locked myself in the bathroom. I stared in the mirror. My face was out of focus. I was only half a person, not even that. I didn't exist. To some man out there, I wasn't even born. I was nothing.

I'd forgiven Holly a truck-load of crap behaviour because I thought she got ditched – being a single mom is tough. But all along it was *her* decision. She'd kept my father from me.

I pull on the manky school dress and join Holly in the lounge. It's so much more than just a lounge. Hell, yeah! It's also a kitchen, dining room and TV room. It's the kind of space that multitasks – an open-plan room the size of an iPad.

"Well, that's Craig. History." Holly switches off her phone and bites into a peanut butter and jam sandwich.

"You dumped Craig?" I wipe the peanut butter and crumbs off the counter and screw the tops back on the jars. "He was nicer than the last one." On a scale of one to ten, Craig is a three. Her boyfriends don't often make it past five.

Holly sets her sandwich down on the side table. She avoids plates, they lead to washing up. "The dude dumped me. But he had issues."

Holly's boyfriends all have issues. She's got rubbish taste in men. Her type: always good-looking and never any good.

She stretches out her legs and puts her feet up on the arm of the couch. It's a dead person's couch. I take my spot on a dead person's chair, chew on a carrot and stare at the pattern on a dead person's carpet. All our furniture comes from the Hospice shop, a lot of our clothes too. The ones that really creep me out are those with a name written on the inside of the collar. Always grimy with some dead person's neck grease.

Holly frowns at her toes and picks at a nail. "I might be late tonight. You'll buy some groceries on your way home from school? I'm not sure I'll get it together."

Holly and I are a partnership and the household chores are split down the middle. She does the splitting and she's not so hot with maths. Seriously, this partnership is no longer working for me. Aunty Agony needs to stop agonising and get back to me ASAP. When I find my father I never want to see Holly again.

I grab my satchel and my lunchbox. I'm going to be late for school. (Thanks, Holly, for coming home at three and waking me up. Lost your front door key. Again?) I scribble a note on my exam pad. *Jenna woke up with a sore throat this morning and I thought she should sleep in. Please excuse her for being late.* I pass the note to Holly but she waves it away. "You do it," she says, licking jam off her fingers.

I sign the note and tuck it into my blazer pocket. "You not working today?"

She yawns. "Just a bit of admin and a pamphlet round. The market is totes rubbish these days."

If you spoke to Holly on the phone you'd think you were speaking to a teenager. There's only one word for it: pitiful.

Holly's an estate agent – one of the million jobs she's had

over the past fifteen years. For now, she sells houses to families who are looking for "real homes". Funny, that. Mostly she doesn't sell. Just another thing she's useless at.

Here's her selling pitch – it's genius: "If you move the couch away from the wall you'll spot the damp. Believe me, under this new paint job the walls are dripping wet. The pipes are rotten." She beats the honesty is the best policy to a pulp. By the time her sole mandate's expired the seller's already lined up another estate agent he can trust to lie.

"I can't help it, baby. I don't like to mislead people." Like that crook who sold us our leaky shack eight years ago.

I leave Holly picking at her toenails and check my appearance in the bathroom mirror. I suck in my cheeks and stare at my reflection. I arrange my hair into a messy bun and use an earbud to smudge my eyeliner. I scan my teeth. All good. I practise smiling, not just with my mouth, but with my eyes. It's Holly's smile, flirty but fun. I try frowning instead.

In the lounge, Holly stretches up her arms to me. Her hugs are always fierce. "I love you more than all the stars in the sky."

I pull away. Hating her.

"More than all the planets in the universe," she says.

Outside, the rain has stopped and the sun screams down at me from a sky washed clean and blue. This is the way of Joburg summers. This city doesn't do things half-heartedly. You want a thunderstorm, Joburg will give you one. You want sun? Don't forget your sunscreen.

On my way to school I pass the *For Sale* signs outside the houses. *Real Homes* say the signs, with photos of Holly grinning at me. She's wearing a dead person's glasses, even though her eyesight is twenty-twenty. It was my idea: Like, get real, Holly. Who wants to buy a house from someone who looks like a cheerleader?

The security guard outside the red brick building opens the gates and lifts the boom.

No firearms or alcohol are permitted on the school premises. Spot tests for drugs will be conducted at the discretion of the school. Underneath this, a *No Smoking* sign.

Welcome to St Virgilius. Virgins, as me and my fellow inmates call it. Not that we'd confess to being saintly or virtuous even if you beat us over the head with a crucifix.

I hand in my note at the secretary's office. She's on the phone but raises an index finger. "Camp fees, Jenna. They were due last week."

"I'm sure my mom already paid." Ha! No chance of that. People who can't sell houses don't have a lot of cash. "I'll get her to call you." I duck out.

I fetch some books from my locker, head for the classroom, and run a hand down the side of my dress. I shortened the hem last week and it's halfway up my thighs. I've got good legs. Holly's legs. I open the classroom door and try to slip past the teacher in front of the whiteboard.

Andile Skhosana turns around as I reach my desk.

"Nice of you to join us." The heat rises in my neck and into my cheeks. Someone sniggers.

"See me after class." He turns back to the board.

See me after class. See me after class. The words beat a tom-tom in my chest. He said it like it was a date. Sort of.

After class, I hang around at my desk. My hands are damp and I have this terrible urge to scratch my left eye. I rub like mad and, too late, I remember the eyeliner.

Panic!

My knuckle is smudged black, so I rub the other eye to balance out the weird panda look. Andile glances up and beckons, his finger crooked. The last girl leaves, shutting the door behind her.

It's just Andile and me. Alone.

"I've got a note from my mother. It's this flu that's being going around, I haven't been able to shake it."

He riffles through a pile of papers, his head down, not looking at me. His hair is thick and springy, overdue for a cut. He's not one of those men who's going to go bald when he gets old.

Maybe I could touch it. Just softly.

"It made me late for class. I'm sorry."

He looks up and smiles. There's only one word for him: snack. No, scratch that. He's a full meal. Andile Skhosana is hot. Sizzling. On a scale of one to Michael B Jordan, he's an eleven. Think Chadwick Boseman meets Childish Gambino – without the boep – and you get the idea. His teeth are straight. But not in that fake way from wearing braces. So I guess he didn't wear them as a child. And the scar on the side of his hand tells me he cut himself, maybe with a knife. It's an old scar, though, and probably happened when he was a kid.

"Oh no, it's your essay I wanted to talk to you about. I handed them back at the beginning of the lesson." He finds my essay and passes it to me.

His voice is Morgan Freeman and his accent murmurs private school. I haven't found out which one. He tends to end his sentences with a question mark, even when he isn't asking a question, as though he's interested in my response, even when I'm not expected to make one. It's like we're having a real conversation.

"It was good, Jen. You really seemed to go the extra mile." He smiles again. This time his mouth is closed, so I don't see his teeth.

I clutch the essay. He calls me Jen. I like the way his tongue touches the top of his palate when he says it. Like a caress.

Jennnnnnnnn.

"What do you mean, extra mile? I ran a marathon for this essay."

He laughs and shakes his head. "Funny girl, Jen."

I look down so he can't see the stupid grin on my face. I made him laugh! I'm funny girl Jen. Not needy, whiney, pissed-off Jenna. I'm different when I'm with him. Brilliant, funny.

"It was like you got inside their skin. It's a real talent."

I shrug. "I love history."

I love you.

"If you ever want to read more on the Second World War, I've got loads of books at home I could lend you."

Andile lives in a flat in Killarney. I saw this on his phone bill while snooping through his classroom desk last month. And I've gone round to the block to check it out. His fifth-floor view of the skyline is brilliant. The flats are selling for more than two million. *Great views. Located near the shops and Gautrain,* the advert says. One day I'll get to see inside his flat.

He is new at Virgins this year, and it's his first teaching position. He studied to be a lawyer at university but the law and him didn't work out. From what he's told us, I guess he had a problem defending crooks and bastards. History's his passion now.

The whole class is in love with him, me most of all. He's twenty-eight and he's got two hundred and fifty-three friends on Facebook. I'm not one of them, but his security settings are rubbish – like most people's.

"Everything all right at home, Jen? You're looking a bit dark around the eyes. Nothing troubling you, I hope?"

I shake my head as the door opens and a girl shoves her face inside the room. Xoliswa is my ride-or-die homie. We've been as tight as a pair of True Religion denims since nursery school. Her hair is a giant afro. No more pretty corn-rows or braids. Natural, she calls it, and refuses to tie it up, even when threatened with detention. She does shave her legs, though. There are limits to natural, obvs. I flash her my death stare: Go away. She gives me a stink eye and ducks.

"Don't be late for your next class." Andile walks me to the door, his hand poised above my shoulder. Not touching, but nearly.

Please, please, touch me – but he never does.

Soo Ling is waiting for me in the corridor. She's the third wheel in my friendship with Xoliswa. She balances us out, but sometimes slows us down. Soo Ling and Xoliswa are pretty much my only friends at Virgins. I'm picky about who I hang with, okay?

"C'mon, Jenna, what did Randy Andy want?" Soo Ling says. "Tell me, tell me!"

We hurry towards the maths class.

"He likes me. He says I'm smart and I make him laugh. He sort of nearly touched me." I give a slow nod. Oh, yes. "And I almost stroked his hair. It's springy and soft. Gorgeous, like a poodle's."

Soo Ling slaps me on the arm and giggles. "Hey, girlfriend, don't let Xoliswa hear you say that. Andy's not a dog, you know." She glances over my shoulder at Xoliswa, who is collecting her books from the locker. "And then what happened?"

"Xoliswa kind of interrupted us just when things were getting interesting."

Soo Ling rolls her eyes at me and pokes the side of her mouth with her tongue. "Yeah, yeah," she says.

I can't help noticing the pores on her chin. I'm sure they've always been there, but for some reason they irritate the hell out of me today.

"What's 'Yeah, yeah'? He invited me around to his flat. This weekend." So, I lie. It's not a biggie. He did sort of invite me round to borrow some of his books. Sort of.

"Shuddup! He never did. You're such a liar!" Soo Ling nibbles at her bottom lip.

"Suck my hairy balls, biiitch." There are some days when I think our friendship has reached a dead end. It's like the longest-running soapie on TV.

"Well, are you going? That's if he really asked you?"

"Maybe. Just don't say anything. Especially not to Xoliswa."

Xoliswa's developed a God complex lately, always judging. Last week when she saw me giving the security guard my school sandwich she'd picked a stupid fight about it.

"What's this, Jenna? An attack of white guilt?"

"Jeez, man, take your head out of your arse. He's poor and hungry, he appreciates it, okay?"

"Really? Have you ever asked him? Why do you people always make assumptions about people of colour? It's so patronising. If he was white you'd never dream of doing it."

For some reason I'd become "you people" instead of Jenna, her best friend. And she was one of them, the "people of colour". Like part of a rainbow that didn't allow white. Things were awkward between us. Everything I said was wrong. We danced around each other, mostly out of step.

Soo Ling and I reach the classroom. But before I open the door

I whisper, "So don't tell Xoliswa, okay? It can be our secret."

Secrets. I knew how to find them and how to keep them.

Holly's still home when I arrive back from school. She's curled up on the couch with *MasterChef Australia*. Those who can't cook watch the food channel. It makes them feel better about being unable to boil an egg.

"You just caught me, baby. I'm off in a couple of minutes."

I'm no longer in the mood to play nice with Holly. "Why haven't you paid the camp fees? If you don't pay, I can't go."

Holly pulls her mouth down and makes her eyes wide like a puppy. "Ag, sweetie, I'm strapped for cash at the mo'. It's been a tight couple of months." She flips herself off the couch and slips on her heels. She still hasn't got around to taking the price sticker off the sole.

"Come on, Jenna, who wants to go on a school camp? Bo-ring!"

Andile's one of the teachers taking the Grade Tens to the Magaliesberg next week. I want to strangle Holly for messing this up for me. Not just camp – my life. Everything.

The conversation doesn't end well. Holly rushes off on her date with a blotchy face, slamming the front door. "I'm a useless, terrible mother and I don't blame you for hating me. But really, baby, I try so hard ..."

A few weeks ago I'd have been more understanding. But I'm done with this woman. I clean up the kitchen (how many coffee cups can one person use in a day?), and load the washing machine.

The telephone rings. Yes, we have a landline. Holly's Plan B for when she breaks/loses/drops her phone in the bath. It will go straight to voicemail and Holly will deal with it when she gets home.

Nope, this is not how it happens. Setting up voicemail to take her business calls is just another small detail Holly will get to when she has time. If it's not someone trying to sell me an insurance policy from a call centre in Pondicherry, it's one of Holly's clients with questions about a house. It stops ringing, and a few minutes later, rings again. I answer.

"Hello, may I speak to Holly Moore?" The woman's voice is hoarse. It belongs to a life-long smoker or someone who's got a chesty cough.

"She's not available right now. This is her daughter, Jenna, speaking. Can I take a message?"

"Jenna? What sort of name is that?" She says this with a snort. "Would you tell her that her Aunt C-C called and she must ring me back? Let me give you my telephone number."

I've never met Aunt C-C or spoken to her on the phone before. Getting a call from her is about as rare as spotting a black rhino in a shopping mall, or a game park. She's somehow related to my great-grandfather Frank. When Holly was fourteen, her parents were killed in a car accident. My mom was a little short on relatives, so she got dumped on Aunt C-C. After Holly got pregnant and dropped out of university, the two of them argued. They've only seen each other a handful of times in the past fifteen years.

Tapping her number into my phone, I say, "Are you sure

there's nothing I can help with?"

"I simply wanted to inform your mother that I intend to put the old house in Pembroke Street on the market. I still have a few of her belongings and I require some assistance with packing up."

Not so interesting. Packing up is grunt work. I've done it for Holly's clients a couple of times and it's something I try to avoid. But I just *have* to be on that bus to the Magaliesberg next week.

"I'm your guy. But I don't come cheap."

"Excuse me, who's 'your guy'? Do you have to speak like some cliché out of a movie?"

Sheesh! Talk about a humour by-pass. It takes a few minutes to agree on a rate. Aunt C-C drives a hard bargain and doesn't allow our blood ties to influence the arrangement. I make sure she agrees to pay me in advance. I start tomorrow.

While we're busy closing the deal, I check out the photos on the passage wall. In mismatched frames, they're arranged Holly-style, a haphazard mess. Among them is an old black-and-white one taken at the house in Pembroke Street. People posing on the stoep. I recognise my great-grandfather Frank. Holly and I have his eyes. His arm is draped around someone who looks like his older brother. Not as hot, though he has the same cheekbones. Daniel – or David, Holly isn't sure. His two daughters are sitting on a step in front of them.

"Tell your mother to ring me," says Aunt C-C. "She must collect the personal things she left behind. And don't you be late tomorrow." She slams the phone down without hearing me say I'm always on time – unless Holly's been messing me around, of course.

I make popcorn for supper and lie on my bed, checking out Andile's Twitter feed. He's watching the soccer, Manchester United. Soccer sucks, but I download some info and memorise the players' names. We'll chat about soccer after class tomorrow!

In the morning, I don't tell Holly about the phone call. Or that I'll be working for Aunt C-C after school. Let's just say that Holly's personal stuff at the big house is something I've got a keen interest in.

On my way out, I glance at the photo of the family at Pembroke Street. I guess from the style of the clothes that it was taken more than fifty years ago. The older of the two girls is wearing a black beret, and she's scowling at the person behind the camera.

I look closer at the girl's face. Her expression is more than just sulky, it's angry. But the younger of the two girls is smiling, mouth closed. She's hiding something behind those sly lips. And the door to the big house is shut, the family gathered in front, like they're guarding a secret.

I'll be there today after school to claim mine. Because if there's anything in Holly's belongings about my father, I'll find it.

MARGARET

Lucy's got long red fingernails and smokes Texan plain. Sometimes a scrap of tobacco sticks to her lips, which are the same colour as her fingernails. She picks it off, often spits it out. Pffft.

My sister's honey-blonde hair hangs like open curtains around her face, which is pale as the moon. She wears a black beret on the side of her head and acts like she's as beautiful as Yvonne Ficker, our Miss South Africa with the perfect 36-24-36 figure. I think Lucy's prettier because her teeth don't stick out like Yvonne's.

"Where is she, Mima? I'm going to wring that brat's neck." Lucy's in a rage. Her words are clipped to an inch, like our privet hedge.

Lucy's got a hot temper and wears short skirts. She can be wild. Too loud. Too fierce. She likes to argue, especially with my parents. When things get nasty my mother grabs her head and goes to lie down. My father chips in with: "Really, Lucy, do you have to provoke your mother? She's not well, as you know."

This makes Lucy even angrier. She's quiet as death, and her top lip curls.

I'm sitting as silent as a mouse under the kitchen table, my legs drawn up. Clumps of faded bubblegum are stuck underneath. They look like the brains of dead rats.

"What's that girl done now?" Gemima says. I spy her black feet, and, as she steps away, a peep of white sole. Her heels have flattened the backs of my mother's old takkies. She turns to stir the Maltabella, making it thick like mud. When it's ready, she'll add milk and brown sugar. It looks better than Jungle Oats, which is like cat sick. Still, I close my eyes as I eat it.

Lucy sucks on her cigarette and breathes out a long sigh of smoke. "She took my fountain pen again. This time she filled it with lemon juice. She's going to ruin it. Seriously, Mima, I'm going to talk to Daddy about her if she doesn't stop her nonsense."

Toughees! My father has already eaten breakfast and gone to his consulting rooms near the Johannesburg General Hospital. He likes an early start. This means Gemima starts early too. Before my father gets up in the morning, she's already put a pot of water on the stove for porridge.

As soon as she hears the sound of his feet on the floorboards and the bath water running, she comes upstairs and gets me out of bed and dresses me for school. While my father eats his oats she cooks him his two eggs and bacon, which she serves with a slice of white toast. Gemima's mummy used to make him exactly the same breakfast when he was a boy on the farm in Natal.

Lucy stubs out her cigarette, squashing it into the ashtray

with sharp jabs. She clips on her earrings and goes outside to wait for Roger the Dodger. He's been Lucy's boyfriend for the past six months. Roger drives a clapped-out Morris Minor which doesn't have indicators or windscreen wipers. My father calls it the red devil.

Roger is studying to be a lawyer. When he graduates he'll have to cut his hair, stop shouting his mouth off about the natives, and learn to toe the line, my mother says.

Lucy is nine years older than me. When she's in a good mood she allows me to sit on her bed and watch her get ready for her dates with Roger. Sometimes she practises the cha-cha-cha on me and lets me paint her toenails. Lately she's been telling me I'm a big pain in the neck and I must buzz off.

Lucy is studying for a Bachelor of Arts at the University of the Witwatersrand but she spends most of her time not studying and raising hell with Roger. My mother says it doesn't matter if Lucy fails her degree because after university she'll probably just get married and won't have to work. Lucy says my mother is stuck in the Dark Ages.

Roger's car backfires as it drives off, and Gemima peers under the table with a smile. "Oh, there you are." She makes me stand still as she sponges the grubby marks off my gymslip. She squints at the shine on the serge. "You can't go to school like that."

She gets her Special Book out of the kitchen drawer and pages through it. I look over her shoulder. "What does Ann say?" Ann Wise's advice in the *Sunday Times* is the only part of the newspaper Gemima reads. When my father is done with the paper, Gemima cuts out Ann Wise's tips and sticks them in my old school exercise book.

Ann knows a stack about lots of things: how to cure warts, remove perspiration marks and any stain under the sun. She's brilliant when it comes to making a can of pilchards stretch to a satisfying family meal. One of Gemima's proudest moments was when Ann published Gemima's "housewives economise" tip on what to do with old bits of soap.

"Scrubb's Ammonia," Gemima says, and unlocks the cupboard door. She chooses a bottle from her collection of household cleaning supplies. Bottles of Ann Wise potions fill her cupboard. She rations my JIK, and it's never enough to clear the inkblots in my exercise books.

During the day she keeps the cupboard key on a string around her neck and at night she hides it in a secret place. I've searched everywhere but I've never found it. My father says the contents of Gemima's cupboard could blow a hole twice the size of Kimberley's in our back garden.

After sponging my uniform, Gemima spoons dollops of Maltabella into a bowl and grabs *Anne of Green Gables*. "You'll mess your nice book." She puts it back on the shelf and watches me eat. "Just one more mouthful." I open my eyes and make hamster cheeks at her. Porridge spurts out of the sides of my mouth and she clicks her tongue and says, "Wena!" (That means "You!" in Zulu.)

I speak the language like a real African because Gemima talked Zulu to me from the time I was a baby. We sometimes chat in Zulu, but Sister Columbanus says I mustn't speak native at school.

"Don't backchat me, young lady. I do not want to hear, 'My father also speaks Zulu, so there.' No, don't dare say that, miss. You are very bold." Sister Columbanus grips the rosary at her belt, like she's seeking support from a higher being.

Breakfast finished, I go upstairs to my parents' bedroom while Gemima makes my school sandwiches. My mother's bed is farthest from the window and the curtains are closed.

"Good morning, Mummy, how are you feeling today?" I speak in whispers. If I talk in my normal voice she tells me not to shout, it hurts her head. Bottles of pills are lined up on my mother's dressing table next to a photograph of her and my father on their wedding day. My mother has a huge grin on her face in the photo. It was a time before the disappointments, when she still knew how to smile.

She raises herself from the bed and presents her face for a kiss. "Don't smother me, Margaret." Her skin is sticky and I can taste the Pond's night cream on my lips.

"I think I may get up today." There's a frog in her throat. My mother often thinks about getting out of bed to sew. But then she pulls the covers up under her chin and sleeps away the day until supper time.

My mother has nerves. She didn't always have them. They came a few years after Lucy was born, when my mother suffered her disappointments and had to spend lots of time recovering. There were four disappointments until I came along. I don't think I made up for them because my mother still spends a lot of time trying to recover.

Gemima laces her walking shoes and takes me to school. I plonk my hat on my head. St Virgilius says it's a mortal sin to be seen in public without a hat. In winter, it's the black felt hat, in summer, the white straw boater. Both are crosses I must bear.

Gemima huffs and puffs like the big bad wolf on the way to school. Every few steps she stops and coughs because she says her cold has gone to her chest.

I take a squizz at her head and wonder how much of her brain the tokoloshe has managed to eat these past few nights. The skin on her neck above the collar of her uniform glistens with Vicks VapoRub. Gemima says the Vicks, along with the Stearns Pine-tar and Honey cough mixture should do the trick. But I don't think so. After tonight, there'll be nothing left of her brain.

Gemima won't let me run ahead, and she coughs and snorts when she hands me my suitcase at the school gate where Benny is waiting for me.

"Slow coach, slow coach, slow coach," he yells.

I grab his wrist and twist, giving him a Chinese bangle to make him stop.

Benny and I are at the same school because the boys' school down the road burnt down last year and they've got nowhere else close by until it's rebuilt. My school is bearing this annoying cross by seating the boys on the left-hand side of the classrooms and trying to ignore them.

The girls sit on the right-hand side, away from the windows, so we boil in summer. It isn't any better in winter because St Virgilius doesn't believe in heaters or spoiling children.

My desk mate is Louise Daincroft. I sit at the front of the class because the teachers say they like to keep an eye on me. Louise sits in the front because she wants to be teacher's pet. She also can't see the blackboard and has to wear glasses that are held on with an elastic so her hair bushes up at the back. Mostly she leaves her glasses at home because she doesn't like me calling her Goggles.

Whenever a teacher needs someone to go outside and beat the blackboard duster with a ruler, Louise flings her hand in the air and shouts, "Me! Me! Me!" She's a champion schloep. I just wait for a teacher to choose me, but they never do because I'm not one of their favourites. Sister Mary Liguori says I am far too bold, always wanting to be the bride at every wedding, the corpse at every funeral.

My Afrikaans teacher's name is Miss van Tonder and she wears skirts and twinsets in summer and slack suits in winter. The jacket covers her bottom because the school doesn't want us to see the shape of a teacher's bottom, or even know she has one.

The rest of the teachers are nuns. They cover up so well you can't even see the colour of their hair. Their faces are squashed like pink marshmallows by a white doek thing they call a coif, and a black veil covers their heads. We call them penguins.

Us girls also have a dress code. Some mornings, Sister Athanasius makes us kneel down to check the length of our dresses. The hem must be exactly four fingers above the knee. Otherwise God will strike us down.

We have to wear huge bloomers that match our uniforms. They make our bottoms feel big. The elastic pinches the tops of our thighs and leaves a pink zigzag on our skin.

When we have inspections, the penguins make us do somersaults in the gym. If we're wearing the wrong broeks we get a hundred lines. Last year Benny dared me to go without any, so they sent me home. I had to write "I must not behave like a heathen" two hundred times and my parents were called in by Mother Superior and told about my wicked tendencies. And my first Holy Communion was postponed. My mother still gets cross when my father jokes about it.

We are also strictly forbidden to chew bubblegum because it's common, and if we get caught the penguins stick it in our hair.

At break time I meet Benny in the quad. "What you got?" I say as I unwrap my sandwich. I fold up the wax paper. Gemima says waste not, want not, but I give it a rip because using the wax paper a second time is horrible.

"Hell's vomit. And you?" Benny says.

"I'll swap you my Peck's for your Hellmann's."

Benny groans. "Jislaaik, that Gemima's got it in for me. She knows I hate fish paste worse than sandwich spread." He offers me half. I take it and hand over my whole sandwich. I snatch his other half. Fair's fair.

Sister Francesca often does surprise lunch inspections. If we don't have sandwiches, she sends us across to the convent kitchen where the cook gives us brown-bread doorstops with no butter, only marmalade, as bitter as her mouth.

The meanest penguin is Sister Columbanus. She teaches us English and hates boys, Benny in particular, who struggles to read and can't spell for toffee. I suppose his Mavis didn't allow him to crawl either.

I'm the best speller in my class. I learnt to read long before I started school by copying out the names on labels. Gemima taught me how. Dr Mackenzie's Veinoids. Anadin. De Witt's. And my mother's favourite: Dr Williams' pink pills for the treatment of tiredness, irritability, depression and nerviness.

Sister Columbanus hits Benny with her ruler when he gets his spelling words wrong. She uses the metal edge of the ruler. The backs of Benny's legs are sometimes covered in cuts, and his mother has to put Mercurochrome on them.

Benny makes the last part of her name sound like a rude word. Columb-Anus. The one time I called her that, Gemima washed my mouth out with Sunlight soap.

After school, I wait for Gemima. Mostly I walk home with Benny, but today she's taking me to Fairplays Haberdashery in Louis Botha Avenue to buy some gingham and thread for my sewing project. I'm going to make her an apron and embroider *Gemima* on the front.

I sit on the pavement outside the school gate. The blue sky is ironed flat with no clouds and the sun makes me hot. I pull off my tie and shift about, but my bottom feels cold.

Sitting on concrete I run the risk of getting piles, also known as haemorrhoids. Gemima's going to be in for the high jump when I tell on her.

I've almost given up when a Morris Minor pulls up. The back of the red devil's window is covered in peeling stickers: *Charge or Release. Remember Sharpeville. Coke is Life.* It's a real student car, one helluva mess, my father says. Lucy leans out the window. "Get in."

I climb into the back of the car. "Where's Mima?"

"Your mother's at home," Roger the Dodger says. The car jerks as he drives off.

"No, not her. Ge-Mi-Ma." I roll my eyes but Roger doesn't see. In any case, he's taking skelm peeps at Lucy's legs.

Lucy turns around, a worry line on her forehead. "Mima couldn't fetch you today. She's at home in bed. It's that cough of hers. It's got really bad."

"Why don't you take her to hospital? To Baragwanath?"

My sister's top lip curls. "Don't be dumb, Mags. Daddy will see to her when he gets home. She'll never get proper treatment at an African hospital."

Cold cement seems to fill my chest. It's all my fault. Between the tokoloshe and me, we've killed Mima.

Roger sticks a thumb out the window and turns right. When we go left, his fingers stir the air, going round and round in a circle. At last he pulls up outside our house. He comes round to my side of the car and lets me out. It's not because he's a gentleman – the door handle is broken and won't open from inside.

I race up the driveway to Gemima's room at the back. She's in bed, propped up on some pillows, and she's wearing my mother's old dressing gown. The wireless my father gave her for Christmas is playing one of her music programmes. She opens her eyes when I throw myself on her. She smells of Lifebuoy soap and Vicks VapoRub.

"Go and soak your shirt in some milk and do your homework." She pats my back. "Those stains won't come out on their own."

I glance down at the blue-stained cuffs and the ink on my hands. My school won't let us use Bics or fountain pens, only the messy old dipping pens. Radiant Blue and I are deadly enemies. Gemima holds a handkerchief to her mouth as she coughs. It's speckled red.

"Lucy's been looking after me nicely all day. Like an angel. When the doctor gets home from work he'll fix me up. Go on, I need to rest."

I leave Gemima and fetch a book from my father's study. *Dorland's Illustrated Medical Dictionary,* his birthday present to me last year. I page through, searching for blood in the mucus – hemoptysis. Gemima either has tuberculosis or pneumonia. Dorland's can't decide.

I get my rope from my bedroom and skip up and down the street until the sweat makes me itchy under my pigtails. I toss my rope on the crazy paving and go next door to Benny. We don't have a wall between our two houses, and I'll sneak in the front door. Maybe I'll surprise Benny. Scare the pants off him. But he's already lying on the front lawn.

"First touch, Scumbucket." I punch him on the shoulder. He's got a pair of binoculars around his neck and he's sucking something.

"Gimmee!" I snap my fingers at him and he passes me the paper bag. I take a black ball out of the bag. "So what colour's your nigger ball?"

"Ag man, Mags. I've told you not to say that word."

"Ball. Ball. Ball. Ball." I chant and leap over him. Jump back. Over again.

Benny catches my foot as I jump and I topple onto the grass. "Not that word. Jislaaik, Mags, why do you always have to be so aggravating?"

We lie on the grass, sucking in silence, trying not to bite. Our tongues change colour, from green to pink, then white.

Waiting.

I'm waiting for my father to come home and fix Gemima. Benny's waiting for his father to come back from his architect office in town. He waits for him most evenings, checking the pavement with his binoculars. The 15b Sandringham drops Mr Schaumbacher off in Louis Botha Avenue, and it's a five-minute walk home. When Benny sees him, briefcase in hand, he runs to meet him.

If Benny doesn't get sight of him by five-thirty, he gets fidgety. It's already long past that. His freckles are smeared across his white face like he's been splashing in a mud puddle.

"Any sign of your dad? I wonder if he missed the bus." Mrs Schaumbacher switches on the stoep lights, settles a tray with two glasses of Fortris on the grass, and glances at her wrist. "It's nearly ten past six. He's not leaving much length for a hem."

Like my mother, Mrs Schaumbacher is a keen seamstress. So she often talks like this. Benny and I work out what she means, then try to copy it. "His bobbin is running short of thread," I say. But Benny's not in the mood.

Mrs Schaumbacher chews the colour off her lips and peers across the low privet at a lime-green Beetle parked under a street lamp across the road. "There's three of them today. Not just the usual two." She gives a jerky wave. "Yes, I know you're there."

"You got visitors?" I look at the car.

She doesn't reply, just shakes her head and sighs.

At the sound of an engine I leap up. My father's black Chevy is pulling into the driveway. "See you later, alligator." I punch Benny on the shoulder. "Last touch." I run off home.

My father gets out of the car and reaches onto the back seat for his hat, his jacket and bag. He's not alone.

"You better get home fast, Mr Schaumbacher. Benny's having an absolute conniption."

"A conniption indeed." Mr Schaumbacher gives a faint smile, tugs at his beard, and checks his watch. "No, I just made it." He stares up the road at the green car outside his house and watches as it goes off. "Thanks Doc, I would have been late if you hadn't picked me up in the main road. You saved my hide."

I drag my father round the back of the house. He must come and fix Gemima.

In the evening, after supper, I slip outside to the back room. The light bulb hanging from the ceiling is on, and it swings when I open the door. The shadows make my father's face look old. He's sitting on a chair next to the bed, a newspaper on his knees. He lifts a finger to his lips.

"Go to bed, she'll be fine."

Gemima is lying as still as someone playing a game of statues.

"Are you sure? Is it the tuberculosis?"

"It's the same thing she had last year, Mags. Pneumonia," he says. "I'll make her better. I promise."

I shift the newspaper and plonk myself on my father's lap. I breathe in his lovely smell: English Leather, Ransom Select cigarettes and Brylcreem. He lets me read the comic strips. Blondie and Donald Duck are my favourites, but my father is mad for Doctor Kildare. I suppose it's because he's also a doctor, although my father doesn't work in the criminal underworld.

I rest my head on my father's shoulder as he reads the news stories out loud to me, his voice low and steady. The dominees are up in arms about the length of ladies' dresses. The short skirts from overseas are the cause of the drought in the Northern Transvaal. My father gives a funny laugh, the one he makes when he's annoyed. He says the dominees are a bunch of verkrampte old fools. He reads more stories, until I don't hear his voice any more.

When I wake up, the winter sun streaming through my window, I'm lying under my bedspread. If Gemima finds me like this she'll hit the roof. She always makes me fold the candlewick bedcover and put it on the chair before I get into bed.

Mima! I leap out of bed and slide down the wooden bannister because Gemima isn't there to shout at me. I rush outside without my slippers on.

My father is still sitting on the chair, the newspaper at his feet. I stand at his side for a while and watch Gemima sleep. Later, I cook the Jungle Oats. While my father eats, I fry him some bacon and eggs sunny side up, the way Gemima does it. After breakfast he checks on Gemima. It makes him late for work.

He comes home early and sits with Gemima through another long night. Until he chases that tokoloshe back to hell.

JENNA

I stand outside the gate of 24 Pembroke Street. What's left of the intercom is hanging from the wall so I can't buzz the house to tell Aunt C-C I'm here.

The dog next door barks, throwing itself at the metal fence as a Neighbourhood Watch guy strolls towards me. He opens his notebook and whips out a pencil. A fifteen-year-old girl in school uniform loitering outside a house. Definitely suspicious. He watches as I take my phone out and make a call.

Aunt C-C eventually picks up. "But you're early. I said three o' clock." She clucks. "Well, all right then. Just give me a moment, I have to come downstairs to open up."

Minutes later, I hear a click and push open the gate. The gravel driveway takes me to the front door of a double-storey house. Water drips from gutters rusted and choked with leaves. Paint peels in damp spots on mottled walls. Potential buyers wouldn't need Holly to point out the flaws.

I skirt a puddle on the stoep and reach the front door. Aunt C-C stands there, a shadowy shape in the doorway. Holly hasn't kept any recent photographs, and I can't say I recognise her. She's Holly's mother's cousin, so she's sort of

Holly's aunt – and my great-aunt, I think. We call her Aunt C-C when we talk about her. Which isn't often.

I wait at the door as her eyes travel down the length of my dress and stop at my thighs. Her eyes narrow. I don't think she likes my hemstitch. I wasn't expecting to be welcomed with hugs and kisses, still, we are kind of related.

"It's lovely to meet you at last, Aunt C-C." I force a smile. Shoot me for lying, but I want to keep the old girl sweet. I really need this job.

"Lovely." She sucks her teeth and grimaces, as if she's tasted something nasty. "Come in, Jenny."

"No, it's Jenna."

"Good lord. What was your mother thinking? Well, come on then, girl." She turns on her heel, then glances over her shoulder at me. "Where's your hat? When I was at St Virgilius, it was a mortal sin to be out in the streets without a boater."

I push my bucket hat further into my blazer pocket. She walks slowly, each step an effort as I follow her into the house. Her candyfloss hair floats around the scaly pink patch on the back of her head. Her skirt hangs loosely at the waist, fastened at the side by a safety pin, as though she's wearing someone else's clothes.

Aunt C-C isn't big on small talk. There's no: "So how *is* your mother? And *you*? What have you been up to all these years?"

"I want you to start in the lounge."

She opens a door off the passage and switches on the light.

"Use the rolls of bubble wrap and make sure each item is secured with tape. I don't want any breakages."

I look around. Ornaments, figurines and crystal glasses fill a mahogany cabinet, and vases and crockery are stacked on the floor. As if someone emptied out the cupboards and dumped everything here.

"Begin with the cabinet and then move on to the rest. Make sure that everything is packed snugly so it doesn't shift around." She points at the bookshelf. "Books don't need to be wrapped, simply place them in boxes. When you've finished, seal the boxes and mark the contents on the outside with the black Koki pen."

"When I'm finished? This is going to take me all year. Where did all this stuff come from?" I edge past a faded floral couch to open the curtains. The chandelier in the centre of the room is missing most of its bulbs, and the room smells musty.

"If you are going to take a year to do just this one room, I will have to consider hiring someone else who works a little smarter."

"I can work smart. Watch me," I say with a smile.

"I think not. I'll be upstairs in my bedroom."

I'm halfway through my second box when there's a thump above my head. I glance up at the pressed-steel ceiling. Fine dust floats down from a crack. Another thump. And a crash.

I leave the room and race up the stairs. Two at a time, counting as I go. Twenty steps. At the top, my shoe snags the carpet. I face-plant and scramble to my feet.

"Aunt C-C, is everything okay?" The passage is dark, and a table stabs me in the thigh. I hit back, and a telephone topples onto the floor.

A door opens and a face peers out. "What are you doing up here?" A sheen of moisture glistens on her skin and she's breathing in gasps.

"I heard a noise," I say. I can't see past her into the bedroom. She clutches the doorframe with both hands, trying to hold herself up. Blue veins bulge on the back of pale speckled hands.

"Go back downstairs to your work and don't stick your nose where it's not wanted." Her voice is harsh, her mouth tight.

So much for: Thank you Jenna, I appreciate your concern, but I was simply practising my pole-dancing moves.

It's an hour later, and I've filled five boxes. I stretch my arms above my head. If I have to touch another piece of bubble wrap I'll eat my left hand.

I cross the threadbare Persian carpet to the bookshelf. My fingers trace the gold-embossed print on the red spines of the leather-bound books. The kind of books no one's ever read, they're just for show. Among them are some photograph albums, maybe with a photograph or two of Holly from the time she lived here and knew my father.

Holly posts her photos on Facebook: Holly and Mike, Holly and Sizwe, Holly the fun-loving gal having the best time ever! Holly's one of my seven hundred and twenty-two friends on Facebook, one of the few I've actually met. But Facebook's for old people, and I don't often post. I'm a lurker.

I reach for the albums and find a spot on the floor. I open one, and dust and silverfish flutter from the pages. They're filled with dead people. From way back. The photos are arranged on black paper, each held in place with white corner pieces. Captions are written in white ink, in longhand. Pretty cool.

The first album begins with a wedding. *David and I on our wedding day. Emmanuel Cathedral, Durban, 6 November 1943.* The bride couldn't have been older than eighteen, about the same age as Holly when I was born. Her plump face is framed by a gauzy veil, and a tiara sits on her head. Totally over the top! She rests her white-gloved hand on the groom's arm. His moustache is carefully trimmed and his army uniform ironed to within a crease of its life. Older than her by maybe five years, he has the hint of a widow's peak. They stand outside a fancy church, squinting into the sun.

The next ten pages are filled with wedding photos. The dimpled bride poses alone in the cathedral garden. *Mrs David Channing-Court at last!* Some group pics. The maid of honour: *Darling Beatrice!* And the best man: *Look, Frank in a suit!* My great-grandfather Frank, the bachelor farmer, long before he got married. Flower girls: *Dearest Gilly and Babs all the way from London.* The mothers, each with a handbag dangling from an arm, glaring at each other like they'd both won the booby prize. The bishop in white robes shakes hands with the groom: *Well done, David! Ellie is a fine young woman!*

I turn the pages. Honeymoon. Victoria Falls, the bride ecstatic, her mouth wide open as spray rains down onto her upturned face. Then she's petting a baby elephant: *Ellie and Baby Ellie! Too adorable!* The groom with a gun, next to a dead lion: *Take that, Simba!*

The newlyweds in their first home. The wife sits on the lawn under a tree, one hand resting on her stomach, an uneasy smile on her face: *Under the jacaranda tree at our new home. 24 Pembroke Street, Johannesburg, June 1944. (The blooms will be glorious in October!)*

Baby photographs. The new mother holds a bundle in her arms, the long christening robe draped over her forearm. The father hovers, a little awkward, but proud: *Lucy two months old. Baptism. The Blessed Sacrament Catholic Church, Johannesburg, February 1945.*

Lucy turns one, then two. I flip the pages filled with photographs charting her life. And then: *Happy eighteenth birthday, Lucy, with pearls from Grandmother Heloise!* Sitting stiffly in virginal white, her skirt a frothy mass that forbids even a peep of an ankle, Lucy looks daggers at me from the page, the pearls like a noose around her neck.

Why are you so angry, Lucy Channing-Court? Did your mother lie to you too?

I page through to the end and open the second album. Another baby! So cute. *Margaret's baptism. The Blessed Sacrament Catholic Church, Johannesburg, April 1954.* The baby is wearing the same christening robe as her sister.

Baby Margaret turns one. The candles on the cake flicker below her howling face. She doesn't seem to like the clown grinning over her shoulder. A maid's apron is captured in a corner of the frame.

A toddler pats mudcakes: *Oh, Margaret, what a mess!* Same kid on a bicycle, with the tip of a shoe behind a wheel: *Daddy teaches Margaret to ride.* A smiling face: *Margaret receives second prize at Sports Day for the egg-and-spoon race.* Then the photos fizzle out.

As I suspected: not a single pic of Holly. I slide the albums back onto the bookshelf. I need to look somewhere else.

Perhaps the chest of drawers? I open the top drawer. A silver-framed wedding photo – like the one I'd seen in the album – lies face down in the drawer. Maybe someone couldn't bear to see it any more. I put it back, face down.

The second drawer is empty except for an old fountain pen, a few paper clips and an unopened pack of extra-strength man tissues – the ones that don't disintegrate after the first blow.

The bottom drawer is stuck. I tug at the handle. Come on, open! Drawers often stick when it rains, but this one seems to be locked. I glance at the open door. It's a risk, but a locked drawer has never stopped me.

I look around, grab a paper clip, straighten it, and slip it into the lock. I kneel down, twist my head to be eye-level with the drawer and poke at the lock.

A door shuts. I prod about as I calculate: twenty stairs at

an old person's pace. Thirty seconds max. I reach inside my satchel for my nail file.

When Aunt C-C appears at the door, I'm standing, duct tape in hand, sealing the fifth cardboard box.

"Well, you've made a start, at least. You're going to have to work a little faster next week." Her eyes glint and she has a wobbly smile. As she walks me to the door, she stumbles and puts a hand against the wall.

"Oopsie-daisy!" There's a grim giggle as I steady her. She allows me to hold her arm as we walk down the passage together.

The sun is dipping behind the koppie, the sky a swatch of pinks from a Dulux paint catalogue. In a few minutes it'll be dark. Joburg draws the curtains closed when you least expect it, shutting out the light.

Aunt C-C stands at the gate, looking edgy. "I don't like you out here on the pavement. Perhaps you should call your mother and tell her you're ready to be picked up." Aunt C-C holds a hand to her mouth. I swear she burped.

"It's no problem, I'm walking. My mother's busy at work."

"Holly? Working? That'll be the day. What's she up to this time? Still temping at that hairdressing salon? Surely not!" She doesn't wait for an answer. "She shouldn't allow you to walk these streets after dark. Most of the streetlights aren't working, you won't be safe."

There's no chance I'm calling Holly. She doesn't even know I'm here.

"Look, Holly's not a taxi, okay? She can't spend her time running around after me. She knows I can look after myself." I sling my blazer over my shoulder and walk down the pavement, leaving Aunt-C-C at the gate.

I head for 37 Klip Street. Holly's been trying to sell this place for ever. It's a corner house close to the highway, which gives it two black marks on the property questionnaire. The advert says: *Beautiful family home. Close to all the best schools.*

What the advert doesn't say is that the beautiful family's home was robbed three times last year. Apart from brilliant thunderstorms, crime's another thing Joburg's good at. I'm not really boasting.

The first time, the thugs got in over the wall of the next-door house. So the beautiful family had bits of broken glass put onto the top of the wall, and an electric fence installed. The next time, the thugs lifted the automated gate off the tracks and waltzed up to the front door. Then the beautiful family put a lock and chain on the gate. But late one night, the thugs hid behind the bougainvillea outside the wall and waited. Her car idling in the driveway, the beautiful wife got out and unlocked the gate. Click. Holding a gun to her head, the thugs escorted her inside.

None of this is in the advert. I only know about it because Holly told me. She tells prospective buyers too, so the house isn't in any hurry getting sold. No one wants a bad-luck house.

The beautiful family has abandoned their home near all the best schools and relocated to a rented flat where they're playing Candy Crush, waiting for the house to be sold so they can emigrate to Ireland and live in a house without burglar bars, electric fences and visits from unwelcome guests.

The first rule every estate agent knows is that people seldom buy empty houses. The rooms echo and don't smell like home. So the beautiful family left the house pretty much as it was, minus a few suitcases. They'll pack up once the sale goes through.

Guards from Stallion Security Company stand outside around the clock to make sure the thugs don't come back a fourth time and clean the house out.

It's Obvious who is on duty today. I'm not kidding, that's his name. He's from Zimbabwe. The guy who does the night shift is Looksmart from Malawi. On their days off, Truelove from Mozambique stands in for Obvious and Looksmart. When Stallion Security gets their guys together for briefings it's like a meeting of the African Union.

I wave at Obvious and he smiles back. He's seen me at the house with Holly and thinks I'm legit. I know the security code and I've got a spare set of keys. Holly keeps them in her office (aka the kitchen) and never notices when I borrow them. Yes, my bad.

There are some people (shrinks, social workers, suckers) who blame bad teen behaviour on upbringing – it's always the parents' fault. Especially the single moms. They'd say that if Holly had given me a father, I wouldn't break into other people's homes to find out what it's like to be part of a family that's not made up of me and a person who doesn't want to be called Mom. Poor little Jenna Moore.

I'm happy to go along with this psychobabble if it gets me off the hook. I'm probably just a weird snoop. Let's keep the verdict open on this, okay?

I slip into the house, punch in the code, and pass the framed photographs of the beautiful family in the hallway: Robert and Dianne Fram, and Katy and James – I've come to know them all by now.

James is eight, and his favourite colour is blue. He's crazy about crocodiles and thinks he's Spiderman: posters of his superhero cover his bedroom wall, stuffed toy crocodiles lie on his blue duvet, with blue cushions on the window seat.

It's James's birthday tomorrow. A folded note in Mr Fram's study drawer says: *Dear Dad, for my birthday I want a cat or a bog, love James.* I suspect James might be dyslexic. I don't think his parents know about this yet, it can be our secret. Sorry, James, we're not allowed to keep an animal in the flat. In any case, it'd be hard leaving it behind when we go to Ireland.

Mr Fram's a great father. He's the kind of dad who does stuff with his kids. Families that play together, stay together. He always wins at rummy, says the score pad – but he's useless at Monopoly. He, Katy and James have been competing in a family Monopoly tournament for a year. Katy's won nine games to James's three. Mrs Fram doesn't play Monopoly, but she's happy to be the bank.

Katy has privacy issues, she's at that age. The sign on her bedroom door says: PRIVATE. KEEP OUT. THAT

MEANS U JAMES!!!! Katy's thirteen, and she's got a crush on a boy called Terence de Villiers. She's written Terence and Katy inside a big red heart drawn on the first page of her school atlas. She's also scrawled *Katy de Villiers* and *Mrs T. de Villiers.* Seriously adorbs! But she'll get her heart broken. The photo stuck on the wall by her bed shows a good-looking boy with eyes set too close together. I know the look: Terence is no good. He'll never look at Katy the way Andile looks at me. The way he looked at me yesterday after class.

I take a book out of my satchel and put it on the shelf among the others: *The Enormous Crocodile* by Roald Dahl. Inside I've written: *Dear James, with lots of love on your birthday. Jenna.* I punch in the alarm code, let myself out.

Back home, I unlock my cupboard drawer and take out a shoebox. The strand of hair is undisturbed. My guard against snoopers. (Note the irony.) It's filled with all kinds of stuff. Katy's hockey badge from when she made the first team. Mrs Fram's perfume bottle. It's empty, but it still has a smell. Cinnamon. I put a fingertip on some things from 3 Frazer Street and 9 Grant Avenue – my other homes.

A shrink could really milk this: *Poor little Jenna Moore steals mementos from other people's houses. She is a sad and seriously disturbed child because she doesn't have a father and her mother is hopeless and a liar.*

Guilty. I am a thief, Your Honour.

I dig around in my satchel for the pile of papers I snatched from the locked drawer in Pembroke Street. An autograph book. So retro, I love it. Maybe I'll get Andile to sign it. I shove it back in my satchel and open a faded report card. The comment on the back says: *Margaret has a vivid imagination which needs to be tempered. She must strive to follow the example of Our Lady and exercise restraint, humility and modesty.*

I put the report in my shoebox, then lift an envelope sticking out from among the papers. *To Aunt C-C*, it says. Inside, there's a lined page, probably from an exam pad. It's torn and the writing is smudged.

I stare at the page. All I can make out is *Danny*. Three other words halfway down: *father* and *my baby*. But my eyes are drawn to one word that stands out clearly: *murderer*.

The eight letters are large and plump. It's Holly's handwriting.

MARGARET

The postbox is overflowing with happiness. So am I.

There are three letters for my mother from her family in England, a medical journal and two bills in brown envelopes for my father, a letter for Gemima – and four letters for me. Australia, Denmark, England and New Zealand!

Dropping the rest of the post on the telephone table, I rip open my mail. I'm careful not to tear the stamps, though. The envelope from Merle Ronaldson in Australia has two blank pages. Yippee, yippee, yay-yay!

"Who they from?" Benny snatches at the paper in my hand, wanting to make a game of it. I pass it over without a fuss.

"There's nothing here." He turns the pages over and scowls. "This is just blank paper." He thrusts it back at me.

"Oh no, my friend. You are so wrong. This is a secret letter. Only I can read it." I run inside and slam the door.

I find Gemima in the laundry, she's sprinkling water on the sheets as she irons. I give her the envelope addressed to *Gemima your girl*. It's from her mother, but it was written by the Indian who owns the shop near Uncle Frank's farm because Gemima's mother can't read or write. Gemima writes back every week, but she doesn't use an Indian. She only finished one year of school on the farm. But she's taught herself to read and write from the Bible.

While Gemima gets busy with her news from home, silently mouthing each word as she reads, I switch the iron on again. It glides over the creamy pages from Australia, and brown writing appears.

I told Merle how to use invisible ink in my second letter to her. Lemon juice or baking soda. I was stuck with lemon juice because Gemima keeps a close watch on her baking cupboard. Lucy's fountain pen works like magic, and when the lemon juice dries it becomes invisible.

I know another way to make secret writing: a clear fluid called urine. Sis! You've got to be mad or desperate to do that.

My eyes flick over the pages. Merle's got a new kitten, her brother had German measles, and her mother has promised Merle's sister a perm for her sixteenth birthday at a fancy hair salon in Brisbane.

I spend the afternoon writing back to Merle and the others. I tell them about Charles, Lucy's cat. He's old and fat now, and my father believes he has kidney problems. He has accidents inside the house. One time Gemima caught him weeing on the breadbin and she nearly had an embolism. I don't tell everyone about Charles's wonky bladder, just that he's obese. I have four envelopes ready for posting by supper time. SWANK. Sealed With a Nice Kiss.

My mother tries to be around in the evenings, even if she's had a perfectly wretched day. An hour before she expects my father home from work, she takes a bath and dresses. She wears stockings, even in summer. She dabs Chanel No. 5 on her neck and wrists and paints her down-turned lips with Revlon's Ice-cream Pink.

My father likes to read *The Star* and have a whisky before we eat supper. My mother always pours it for him: two inches of Bell's and three blocks of ice, no water. She sets the ashtray down next to his chair on a small table alongside the newspaper. His comfortable Hush Puppies wait at the foot of the chair.

Lucy is home for supper tonight. My mother insisted on it, even though Lucy moaned that she was cramping her style. It's a special occasion because my mother is throwing a dinner party. She's also having a complete cadenza because she says Zacharias our garden boy is sick and can't wait on table. Mummy won't have him serving with a dribbling nose and coughing his germs over everyone. She's going to have to make do with Moses, the Schaumbacher's boy, who isn't as well trained as Zacharias. Still, it was generous of Mrs Schaumbacher to lend him to us for the evening.

We're having guests from England, which is a place like heaven, my mother says. Bishop Forrester and his niece are friends of my mother's family in London, and she says Miss Forrester is on the shelf. It means she's old and will never catch a husband.

My Uncle Frank only got married when he was thirty-eight, but my mother says it's different for men. He wasn't on the shelf, he was an eligible bachelor until he got caught by a scheming minx from an old Natal family.

We're all sitting in the lounge, waiting for the guests to arrive. This lounge is never used, it's for special guests and is always locked. My mother keeps her cutglass and Royal Doulton in the mahogany cabinet. Woe betide me if I touch anything.

I am in hell. My twinset is nibbling at my neck, my tartan skirt is scratchy on my legs. My church shoes are pinching my toes. I can't get comfortable on the ball-and-claw couch. I'm not allowed to tuck my feet underneath me because I'll spoil the Sanderson's upholstery. It's come all the way from England. The very best, my mother says.

"Don't," she hisses as I reach for the bowl of cashew nuts on the side table. "Wait until they arrive."

I'm starving, my stomach is rumbling. The grandfather clock in the hallway strikes seven and my mother twists her hands in her lap. Mrs Schaumbacher would say my mother's spool of thread is wound too tight. I'd say she's stretched her elastic too far and it's going to snap.

My mother has spent weeks planning this special evening. She's abandoned Mrs Beeton and has taken up with Elizabeth David. My Aunt Beatrice in London told my mother that Miss David's *French Provincial Cooking* is all the rage and is bound to impress. *Mrs Beeton's Book of Household Management* is now a bit fuddy-duddy. My mother's nerves can only cope being daring with the main course. She's playing it safe with the starter, and, of course, she's serving my grandmother's trifle for dessert – lots of maraschino cherries, walnuts and sweet sherry. It's now my mother's signature dish – she adds her own special ingredient. My mother says we need to make the very best impression and I must mind my Ps and Qs.

To distract my mother from her nerves and my noisy stomach, I tell her the news from Australia. "Merle Ronaldson has a new kitten." I've been hinting about getting a kitten for ages because these days Charles is a poor excuse for a cat.

My mother just nods and says, "We'll see." This is her way of saying no.

The room twitches in the silence. I ask my father for money to buy stamps at the post office after school tomorrow.

My mother sits up even straighter. "I don't think so, Margaret." This is another way my mother says no.

"Quite right," says my father. "I don't want you going to the post office either. It's not safe."

"If you want any letters posted, your father will give Gemima some money and she can go for you."

Next to me, Lucy snorts like a pig. "That's nice. Let Mima get blown up by a bomb."

"Good heavens, keep your voice down, Lucy!" My mother cranes her neck at the open door.

"Well, it's true. If you think there's any risk of the post office getting bombed, why send Mima? Or perhaps you think an African life is worth less than a white one?"

"That's enough, Lucy. Of course your mother doesn't think that. And it's just until things get back to normal."

My mother glances over at Lucy's legs and purses her lips. "Did you shorten that hem? It's at least six inches above the knee." She checks her watch again and rubs her palms together.

Lucy smiles at my mother. "Skirts are a lot shorter in London. I'm sure Bishop Forrester gets to feast his eyes on his parishioners' legs when he delivers his Sunday sermon."

Before my mother can blow a fuse, the knocker bangs on the front door. My father drains the last of his whisky and puts the glass on a coaster. Smack-bang in the middle, the way my mother likes it. "Shall we all support your mother tonight? Not let the side down. Lucy? Margaret?"

My mother casts her eye over the room: the shelf with her leather books, framed family photographs on the bureau, proteas on the coffee table that's exactly in the middle of the Persian carpet. She straightens the wedding photograph, runs the tips of her fingers over the table with the sherry decanter and the crystal glasses, and plumps up a cushion. "Yes, let's all put our best foot forward. Please, girls."

We sit around the dining-room table. It's covered with my grandmother's damask tablecloth, a family heirloom all the way from England, used only on special occasions. My mother rings the silver bell to tell the kitchen we are ready to eat. We always use the bell to call Gemima when we're having supper. Only my mother gets to ring the bell, she never gives me a turn.

While my father pours the grown-ups a glass of Harvey's

Bristol Cream, Moses sets down a serving of avocado ritz –
guests first, beginning with Miss Forrester. Moses is a lot
bigger than Zacharias. He looks miserable in Zacharias's
white jacket, the red sash tight across his chest. After putting
the last plate down in front of me, Moses stands at the end of
the room, even though my mother jerks her chin at him to
go back to the kitchen.

"Perhaps our venerable guest would like to give thanks?"
My mother smiles at Bishop Forrester. "My Lord?" she says.

"Can I? Please can I say it?" I have a new grace Benny
taught me: *Rub-a-dub-dub, thanks for the grub.* My mother
makes slit-eyes while smiling at me with a lot of teeth. It
means no.

We all bow our heads as Bishop Forrester makes the sign
of the cross in the air, his ring flashing purple. Then he says:
"Bless us, O Lord, and these thy gifts, which we are about to
receive from thy bounty. Through Christ our Lord. Amen."

My eyes are closed to a peep. Lucy never shuts her eyes
during grace. She keeps staring straight at my mother, right
until my mother opens her eyes and says "Amen".

Lucy says she doesn't believe in God. When my mother
hears Lucy say this she says her head is about to explode and
she goes and lies down. Lucy's always trying to stir things up
about God and the natives. It upsets my mother, but my
father just laughs and says, "Poor old God. What will you not
believe in next month, Lucy?"

My mother sweeps her eyes around the table as we eat. She
picks her parsley off the shrimp and holds it up. "This grows

wild in a pot by the kitchen door. They say you're a good housewife if you can grow parsley." My father smiles at her and says, "And so you are, Ellie darling."

I don't tell our guests how my mother's parsley died last month and Gemima had to borrow some from Mrs Schaumbacher's pot. Or point out that the avocado is not quite ripe.

My mother makes noises in her throat as we eat. My father asks Bishop Forrester what he thinks about the Wallabies rugby tour – the Boks won a terrific first test match last week. Bishop Forrester says he's a cricket man. Also, he has no view on the Springboks' backline players.

My mother clears her throat again.

Miss Forrester is a timid sort of a person and says very little. Only things like: "I wonder what the weather will be like tomorrow?" Whenever she says anything, she looks at Bishop Forrester and he nods at her like she's answered a multiplication sum correctly in class. My mother quickly passes Miss Forrester the jug when she says, "Sorry to be a nuisance, could I help anyone to some water?" Poor Miss Forrester, we all forgot to offer her some water.

I put my best foot forward and talk to our guests about things I think will interest them. "My friend Benny Schaumbacher says religion is the opium of the masses." I nod towards Bishop Forrester. "That's what Benny says." I catch my mother's eye, and add, "My Lord."

"Opiate. Karl Marx says opiate. Not opium." Lucy gives Bishop Forrester her sideways look and pulls her mouth skew. "My Lord."

"Benny's at school with me this year because his burned down last year. Mine's a convent school. But Benny's father says if there's any chance of Benny turning to Jesus, the penguins will beat it out of him for sure."

I look around the table. Lucy is smiling like a Cheshire cat, and my father dabs his lips with Granny Heloise's best linen serviette as he holds it over his mouth.

Bishop Forrester's eyebrows climb up his big pink forehead. "What an interesting view. And who is this Benny Schaumbacher?"

"He's a … whatchamacallit." My mother looks at Lucy, raises her chin a little. "Jewish," she murmurs.

"Benny's not really Jewish. He eats bacon and he doesn't go to the synagogue. Also, his family gives presents at Christmas, just like us." Last Christmas the Schaumbachers gave me a *Bunty* annual. Benny knows my mother doesn't like me to read books with comic pictures, and over her dead body the ones with real-life photos that the nannies and Afrikaners read. Not people like us, my mother says. But Benny thought no mother would be mean enough to confiscate a Christmas present. He was wrong.

Bishop Forrester runs a hand over his dog collar. "Schaumbacher? That's an unusual name. For some reason I know it. Isn't he …?"

My father nods. "Yes, you may have read about him. He's been in the news quite a bit lately."

"Good gracious me. Margaret's friend is the child of a communist?" His eyebrows climb down again. Slowly. They make me think of my mother's soufflés.

"Lenny's a good fellow and a fine architect. He's been our neighbour for years. In fact, Ellie and Mrs Schaumbacher are close friends, aren't you, dear?"

My mother chews with her lips tightly closed and frowns at my father.

"Best friends, like Benny and me. She's always coming round to help Mummy with her sewing. And she lent us Moses for supper tonight because our Zacharias has a runny nose." I turn to Moses, standing as still as the delicious monster in the corner. "Hey, Moses, how are your sweet peas doing this winter? Ours aren't looking too good – isn't that so, Mummy?"

My mother jerks her head in the direction of the door and says, "Moses, perhaps you could see how Gemima is getting along with the second course." She turns to me and tightens the serviette around my neck. "Careful, there, don't mess."

We're having Elizabeth David's special French lamb dish called Carre d'Agneau. It's really just lamb chops stuck together. My mother taught Gemima how to cook it and has told her to tie a paper doily at the end of each chop bone so it looks like the lamb is wearing a white crown. There's also lots of gravy. Yum, yum, piggy's bum. It has to be served with roast potatoes, peas and one other vegetable. If it's pumpkin, I'll kill myself.

My mother takes a deep breath before speaking. "I am not unneighbourly towards Rachel Schaumbacher. She's a simple soul, and not at all political. I think her husband's activities have caused her a lot of hardship. She's a good wife and supports her husband loyally, which is as it ought to be." She chooses each word carefully, like she's playing a game of pick-up-sticks. Her neck gets blotchy.

"Lenny's a fine bridge player. We so enjoyed our Wednesday-night games with them until we had to stop, didn't we, Ellie?" My father puts his fork down, sips his sherry. "It's illegal for him to be in a gathering of two or more people coming together for a common purpose. Ridiculous, really, as if playing bridge or tennis could be interpreted as treasonous." My father frowns. "At any rate, I suspect it makes running his business jolly tricky."

Moses brings a big tray and puts the lamb on the sideboard with the roast potatoes and the peas. And pumpkin – it's steamed, I can see, so no sugar. The very worst. He sets the warmed plates in front of my mother, who carves the meat. She puts a portion on each plate, which Moses hands to the guests. Between each serving, she dabs at her neck with a lacy handkerchief before tucking it under her watchstrap again. Her hankies always smell of eau de cologne.

When Moses comes round again with the gravy and the vegetables, I notice a smear of gravy on his glove. My mother notices too and starts fiddling with the gold cross at her neck. I take two potatoes to make up for no pumpkin. But my mother spoons some of hers onto my plate.

Moses puts the serving dishes back on the cork mats on the sideboard in case anyone wants seconds. He stands at the side of the room until my mother flicks a finger at him. He goes back to the kitchen, where he'll wait until she rings the bell for him to clear the plates.

"This communist fellow isn't one of those involved in the recent goings-on at that farm near Rivonia, is he?" Bishop Forrester tries to spear a pea, which rolls away. "Our newspapers say that those arrested will stand trial for treason, or at the very least, sabotage."

My father passes me the jug of water. "Lenny is one of many who were acquitted in a long treason trial a couple of years back. But he's still very political, of course. He's been under house arrest for several months, which makes his life rather difficult."

Lucy butts in. "The authorities have told him to report to the police station every day, and he's confined to his home from six-thirty at night until six-thirty next morning. It's barbaric." Lucy has that look on her face, she wants to pick a fight. Not a fight, she always says, a debate.

What Lucy is saying isn't really true. Sometimes in the evenings Mr Schaumbacher isn't at home. When the telephone rings, Mrs Schaumbacher says, "He's busy at the moment in the garage, can I get him to call you back?" I've heard Benny say this too. They never say he's out gallivanting.

I pour myself some water, take a mouthful of pumpkin and a big sip, swirl it around and try to swallow it all down.

"Margaret, please. Don't mix cement." My mother moves the glass out of my reach.

Bishop Forrester looks away. "This Mandela chap has certainly stirred things up. His people need to remember that

Christ rather than communism is the true path to salvation."

There's a loud clunk as Lucy's cutlery falls to her plate. My mother grips her fork as Lucy pushes her plate away and gets up from the table. "Excuse me, Mummy, I'm feeling bilious." I have to agree with my mother, Lucy's skirt is jolly short. Bishop Forrester thinks so too. His eyes don't leave the back of her legs as she walks away.

As Lucy opens the door, Charles slips in and makes a bee-line for the leather pouf in the corner. Leather has become his most favourite thing since my mother put stones in the pot plants. To discourage him, she said. I see him squat, and leap up from the table. "Goddamn you, cat. Take your business outside." Too late.

Bishop Forrester puts down his cutlery. "Some are of the view that children should be seen but not heard," he says with a funny smile. "I see that this is not the case here."

Grabbing Charles by the scruff of his neck, I drag him from the room. I dump him in the kitchen where Gemima is arranging strips of angelica on top of my mother's signature trifle.

Back in the dining room, conversation has dried up again. So I say, "That's Charles. Lucy named him. She'd have called him Anne, but he's a boy cat. Although, he's not a proper boy, because Daddy had his testicles removed."

My mother puts her face in her hands, and she even rests her elbows on the table. Miss Forrester gives half a giggle and covers her mouth. "I don't mean to be troublesome, but does anyone need the salt?" My mother remembers her manners, and quickly passes it to her.

Our guests leave straight after supper. So there's no after-dinner coffee or KWV Brandy. Miss Forrester says no to my mother's offer to share her trifle recipe. She says "no" quite loudly for such a timid person. They leave in such a rush my mother doesn't get a chance to curtsey and kiss Bishop Forrester's ring again. She retires to bed without even washing the crystal glasses. Like she always does after a dinner party, before counting the silver. She says there are some household tasks she trusts only herself to do.

For the next two days she is laid low with the worst of headaches. So low she can't bring herself to get up and bath before my father gets home from work. I put the ashtray right where he can use it without dropping ash on the carpet. And he teaches me how to pour his Bell's. Three cubes of ice. Just how he likes it.

JENNA

Andile Skhosana@JustAndy Shopping
@Killarney Mall. Must get out of bed and grab a
caffeine hit before I get going

So, Andile and I are both still in bed. I know I'm acting like
a crazy stalker, but why would God create Twitter if she
didn't want me to use it? @JustAndy shops at Checkers. He
never does Woolworths. Says the prices are criminal and all
that plastic and polystyrene are a no-no. He's a recycling
junkie. Shops on Saturdays. Goes early to avoid the weekend
mall crawlers. Then a movie. Or breakfast at Mugg & Bean.
It's amazing what people's Twitter feed will tell you about
their lives.

I've been up ever since the first police siren, checking out
Andile's Twitter posts. There's a hollow feeling in my
tummy; I think I'm nervous, or maybe I didn't sleep too
good. Holly got home in the early hours and made one heck
of a racket. She was with Barry. They'd got friendly at the
Tuesday yoga class. I should have known Holly's enthusiasm
for yoga had to be more than just flexibility and inner peace.
Om Shanti Om!

I leave a note on the kitchen table and let myself out. At the end of the road I wait for a taxi. A dog walker drags three bulldogs down the street. One strains at its leash, trying to mark the agapanthus along the verge. The guy gives it a jerk – probably wants to get back to weeding the garden before the boss wakes up.

Earlier on it was threatening to storm, the sky covered by a heavy grey blanket, but now it's a harsh blue. The kind of blue James Fram would like. Happy birthday, James! The sun is hot on my face and I can feel my skin burn. Damn, I've forgotten to put on sunscreen.

I spot a minibus taxi coming down the drag and hold out two fingers. It stops, and I squeeze inside, next to a woman eating pap and chakalaka out of a Tupperware. I watch as she scoops the food up with her fingers. She catches my eye, nods at the open container, but I shake my head. I don't like pap. And I'm not hungry. My stomach is a ball of barbed wire.

The taxi stops, and two more people push their way in. We're way overloaded with passengers on their way to the shops. Soo Ling and Xoliswa aren't allowed to take minibus taxis. Their moms say they're death on wheels, always speeding to make the fare target, and skimping on maintenance.

Holly doesn't have the same issues. She says she's not one of those mothers who drives their kids around. That's for other moms whose kids don't value their independence. Lucky for me I have a mother who doesn't give a flying duck if her daughter takes rides in death traps.

Cars hoot as the taxi makes a sudden stop to pick up yet another passenger. The 4x4s swerve around us, the drivers shaking their heads, faces ugly with rage. They don't yell abuse, you never know when a taxi driver's going to pull out a gun or run you off the road.

Maskandi music thumps all the way to Killarney Mall, with plastic sheeting at the window frip-frip-fripping, and the exhaust vomiting black smoke.

I'm not a big mall fan. There are always too many people walking too slowly. Too many people with too little money buying too much crap they don't need and can't afford.

My chest tightens, I can't ignore the buzz in my ears.

Breathe, Jenna, you can do this.

The Mugg & Bean is packed with families, their plates piled with obscenely big muffins or the M&B Classic breakfast. I scan the faces, walk past the restaurant, and wait at the end of the passage. After five minutes of staring at dead-eyed mannequins in the shop window, I head back to the Mugg & Bean.

A table with a view of passing traffic is free. I wave at the hostess seating the customers: I'm sorted. I grab a chair, pretend to study the menu. I already know what I want to order.

"Just coffee. I need a caffeine hit." I take a book out of my bag and make like I'm reading. I don't see a word, I keep watch on my surroundings.

And then, Andile – pushing a Checkers trolley! A woman bumps into him and he smiles an apology, like it's his fault.

He stops and chats to the hostess. He points to the trolley and they look for a table so he can park his shopping close by. I turn the page of my book and look up.

I'm here, Andile.

At first I don't think he sees me. My hair is free of the regulation school elastics and I'm wearing civvies, my dress arranged to expose my left shoulder. Sometimes you don't immediately recognise people when they're outside of their normal context.

His eyes brighten and he waves in my direction as he says something to the hostess. He parks his trolley and walks over.

"Hello, Jen. Nice of you to keep this spot for me." Andile winks. He's wearing track pants and a faded T-shirt. He's killing that T! *Rhodes Must Fall.* He cocks his head at me. "Would it be too embarrassing for you if your teacher shared your table? Or are you waiting for someone?"

I'm waiting for you, Andile.

I shrug and point at the chair opposite me. "I like your T-shirt."

Brilliant. Come on, Jenna, you can do better than that.

He glances down, as though he's forgotten what he's wearing. "Oh yes, down with Cecil John, down! Nasty piece of work, that one. He left us with quite a legacy." He rubs the side of his jaw, as if he hasn't shaved, or maybe he's just thinking. "Sorry, school's out," he says. "I'll shut up."

Please don't stop. I love your voice.

"No problem. I'm used to Xoliswa banging on about the past – oh, and white privilege, of course. As if I should constantly grovel for being white." I twirl a strand of hair, lean in, widen my eyes – like Holly does. "But it's all a bit crazy. She lives in a really posh house and gets more pocket money than me."

Like, way more. Holly's budget doesn't extend to pocket money.

Andile nods. "You know, she's not the only one who thinks that way. White people can be very arrogant. And dismissive towards black people." He pauses, then looks at me and says, "Maybe you're not really listening to her, Jen?"

Jennnn!

I take a serviette and start shredding it. Seriously, if we don't get off politics soon I'll vomit.

The waitress arrives, puts my coffee down. Phew!

Andile grins. "I see we like the same poison." He looks up at the waitress and says, "Same for me, make it a double shot. And a glass of water, please."

I sip my coffee. It's bitter. I prefer rooibos.

"What are you reading?" he says.

"Only three pages left." I turn the book over, and he reads the title on the cover.

"Anne Frank's diary. Hey, fantastic."

He tells me how last year he'd visited the place in Amsterdam where Anne and her family were holed up, hiding from the Nazis. I smile, my eyes widening again; I'd seen his Facebook photos weeks ago.

When the bill comes he reaches for it, waving away my wallet. I shrug and put Anne Frank back inside my bag. "I

THE CHOICE BETWEEN US

can't stand it when I finish a book and I've got nothing to read." I wait, a hard knot in my tummy. It's been rehearsed in my head. He has to, has to say it. There's no way I'm going to lose face in front of Soo Ling.

He folds a couple of notes into the bill. "I've got plenty of books I could lend you. I live just round the corner."

At last. I'll be going home with Andile.

We walk the three blocks to his flat. He strides slightly ahead of me, his arms swinging the grocery bags. At the corner he stops at the spaza shop operating out of the garage of a house. The woman behind the counter shakes a couple of cigarettes from a box and takes coins from two kids stupid enough to think smoking is cool.

She and Andile chat in Xhosa and she hands him a packet of sour worms. I wouldn't have guessed he has a sweet tooth. Now there's something else I know about him.

He guides me past the superintendent in the foyer. "She's with me, she's a friend. No need to sign in." We head towards the lift.

I'm with Andile. His friend. I'm about to reach for the fifth-floor button, but pull back. Sheesh, Jenna. That was close.

"It's the fifth floor." His hand brushes mine as he presses the button. Going up.

My palms are clammy as I stand behind him at the door to his flat, checking out his pot plant. The leaves are brown at the edges, and the soil is dry. Andile sure doesn't have a green thumb.

I haven't written the script for past the door. My tongue feels swollen, I taste metal in my mouth. As Andile puts the key into the lock and pushes the door open, he is tackled at the knees.

"What you bring me? Where's my sweets? You didn't forget?"

No! He's never said anything about a kid.

I step back as he bends down among the grocery bags and unwraps the hands from his legs. "Hold on, Bonni, time out. This is a student of mine from school." He looks up at me and smiles at the child. "Go on, where are your manners, introduce yourself to Jen."

Brown eyes stare up at me from behind thick glasses. I crouch down next to Andile, smile, and reach out my hand. "Pleased to meet you. I'm Jenna Moore."

"I'm Bonelwa Skhosana and I'm six years old."

"Five, you big fibber. Your birthday's only in three months' time." Andile taps her on the side of the head, like he's making her remember. "If you can guess what I'm holding behind my back, they're yours."

Bonelwa's eyes grow huge behind her glasses. "I guess, Uncle Andy, I guess ... sour worms. My best!" She grabs the packet and races down the passage.

Uncle Andy. Not Daddy. I relax.

A woman pokes her head around the door. "Andy? You back already?" She smiles at me, and it dimples her cheeks. My smile freezes. God, she's pretty. "Oh great, a visitor. I knew there was a reason I made too much batter." She reaches out a hand covered in flour. "I'm Thenjiwe, Andile's sister."

Just his sister.

The morning passes too quickly. We eat amagwinya, it's just like vetkoek, but filled with polony. "Amagwinya ne French – a taste of childhood," Andile says. Polony is nasty, but I pretend to like it. We chat. I make Andile laugh and Thenjiwe makes me laugh harder. She's staying with him for a few weeks until her furniture arrives from Cape Town.

Andile speaks to Bonelwa like she's a proper person and not just a kid. He listens, answers straight. He doesn't use kids as a prop like adults often do to make them look good. I think he speaks to everyone like this. Except, with me it's special. It's the way he says my name.

Jennnnnn.

"That's clever," I say, tapping his coffee mug: *Cool History Teacher is not an oxymoron.*

"He got it on Valentine's Day." Bonelwa pokes Andile in the ribs and giggles. "From his girlfriend."

Andile tickles Bonelwa so she collapses on the kitchen floor. "My guess is Miss Leventhorpe. It's her brand of humour. She's always chewing me out in the staffroom about using her mug. But I brought it home instead. Classic."

I laugh, maybe a bit too loudly. Miss Leventhorpe is my English teacher. She's a hundred years old and smells of onions. She'll be pensioned off at the end of the year and I'm hoping to get someone less uptight. Someone who won't blush when she reads the word "virgin", or "breast".

I trace the writing with my fingertip. I knew Andile would

love it the minute I saw it in the shop last month.

"I spoke to Tata last night. He called five times." Thenjiwe holds up five fingers. "Yes, five." She nods her head at Andile in a shared joke.

"Damn, I missed his call. Has he found a new hobby yet, now that you and Bonni have left town?" Andile doesn't sound sorry, though, more like he's had a lucky escape.

Where was he was last night? I didn't see anything on Twitter or Facebook. I hate not knowing.

"Mama says he's impossible. He's still going on about how I wouldn't have managed the move without his help and how exhausting the whole thing was. Now he doesn't know what to do with himself." She tucks a braid behind Bonelwa's ear, smoothing a hand over her head as she does so. "Hey, Bonni, Khulu's missing us so badly. He's giving Gogo a really hard time."

Andile and Thenjiwe talk about their father in a code only they understand. A mix of love and despair. They're allowed to. They own him. He's theirs. I want to join in and say: "My dad's also a real pain. Like he's always wanting to hang out and do stuff with me." I ache to moan about my father like they do.

Thenjiwe turns to me with a wry smile. "You know what they say about fathers and their daughters. At least I've got three sisters to share the load." She rolls her eyes. So do I. Dads!

"Yeah, Danny's a bit of a control freak when it comes to me. I'm his one and only." A lump of amagwinya lies like clay in my mouth. "You know, Daddy's little girl and all that."

Jeez, Jenna, where's this coming from?

Thenjiwe nods. She knows. But I don't. Was Danny my father? *Murderer?* It's been screwing with my head ever since I read Holly's letter. Driving me nuts. I waited for Holly to come home last night to tackle her about it, but when she and Barry finally got back, they immediately got busy.

After we've eaten, Andile takes me out onto the balcony to show me the view of the Magaliesberg. I hang over the railing as I look at the city sprawled between us and the distant range. I take a few pics with my phone. He leans against the balcony, his back to the view. I stand next to him and hold my phone up but he shakes his head and edges away.

Bonelwa calls out to him. "You said we'd do my new puzzle after breakfast." She struts up to us, and stamps her foot.

"In a minute, Bonni. As soon as Jen's gone home." His eyes are on her. She has his full attention. I shift closer, angle my phone towards him.

Smile. Selfie time.

Click.

Soo Ling won't dare call me a liar again. I'll send her the photo as soon as I get home. It'll be just Andile and me hanging out and having breakfast together. In his flat. She'll die of jealousy.

Andile lends me some books and says I can return them to him at school. But I'll be back for a visit once his guests have gone. Then it really will be just the two of us.

Before leaving, I ask to use the bathroom. I run the cold water while I look around. Andile has a purple toothbrush. He doesn't squeeze the toothpaste from the bottom. He uses body wash from a tube, no soap. I agree, it's more hygienic. A shampoo bottle in the shower. It smells of apple. The cap is on the floor. I resist picking it up and closing the bottle. Never leave tracks, Jenna.

I open the bathroom cupboard. It has the usual man stuff. Spare razor blades, shaving cream, half-full bottles of medicine, roll-on, cough sweets. Tucked behind a box of pain killers is a packet of condoms. Of course, Andile is an adult, he has sex. He's probably done it lots of times.

He will be my first.

MARGARET

My father is taking my mother to supper at a new French restaurant at Zoo Lake tonight. It's terribly smart and she's made herself something special for the occasion. She wanted the same style as a dress Queen Elizabeth wore on her tour to Australia this year. My mother never copies Princess Margaret. She's too racy. She also had her hair done this afternoon. A cut and a perm, but no colour -- that's for shop girls, my mother says.

My father often takes me to Zoo Lake to throw bread crusts at the ducks and watch the coloured lights on the fountain in the middle of the big island. Sometimes we have a picnic under the gum trees and row the boats together. Long ago, the English ballerina Margot Fonteyn danced *Swan Lake* on the small island. Lucy went to see her, but I was only two and had to stay behind, tied onto Gemima's back. Worse luck.

When my parents go out to supper, I usually sleep in the back of the car, parked in the road outside. I take a sleeping bag. It's fun, like camping. But my father says those days of sleeping in the back of the Chevy are over, times being what they are, and so forth.

I'll be staying at the Schaumbachers instead, for the whole night. I'll sleep in Benny's room, he says he'll sleep with his mom. My mother never lets me. She says I wriggle too much. In any case, it's unhygienic. Benny makes it sound like he's doing me a big favour, but I know he sleeps in her bed every night. His Mavis told Gemima. When he sleeps with her he doesn't wet the bed. Lately he's been poep-scared.

Benny and I are drinking coffee, eating Zoo Biscuits and listening to Springbok Radio's *No Place to Hide* with Mark Saxon. He's the investigator who came back from the moon, and he can see horrible things that happen in the future. It's one of the scariest radio programmes and Benny and I are on the edge of the couch with nerves. I always know when there's danger because Mark Saxon smells almonds. After listening to this show, it takes me ages to fall asleep. Every shadow, every noise is out to get me. I love it.

"Can we put the lights back on? I just want to see what animal I'm eating. It tastes like a zebra but I'm not sure. Please, Mags."

"Liar, liar, your pants are on fire. You're just scared. They all taste the same." I've carefully nibbled away at the biscuit part. All that's left is the icing animal. I'll eat it later. Benny just shoves the whole thing in his mouth.

"Fine, but I need to pee. Put the lights on and we can turn them off again after the adverts."

When the jingle for Knorr soup plays I switch on the lamp and Benny shuffles down the passage to the bathroom. I hear the toilet flush so I know he never actually went. He always forgets to flush after he does a number one.

I wait for him behind the door and when he comes back I leap out like Sergei the Russian, my pistol pointed straight at him. "Don't worry, I'm right behind you, Mark!"

Benny squeals, his face like chalk. I nearly wet myself laughing.

"Oh good, you two having fun?" Mrs Schaumbacher stands in the doorway, holding a cup of coffee. A cigarette dangles between two fingers of her other hand. "Straight to bed after *Address Unknown*, okay? No mucking about. No jumping on the bed. Benny's dad is trying to get some work done in his study and doesn't want any noise." She points a finger at me. "You can read quietly. But not too late."

In the middle of the night I hear the telephone. It doesn't stop ringing. Maybe they're all asleep. They haven't left the bedroom light on. My door's open, and Benny's cricket bat's by the bed. I'm jumping up every few minutes to shut the creaky wardrobe door.

I tiptoe to the passageway and answer the phone the way Gemima has taught me: "This is Margaret Beatrice Channing-Court speaking. May I help you?"

"Is Mrs Schaumbacher available?"

"Hold on, she's asleep. I'll call her."

"No. I can't wait. Just tell her: 'Mrs Gray has taken her dog for a walk.' That's all. Have you got that?"

"Mrs Gray has taken her dog for a walk. Yes, what sort of dog has she got?"

"Wake her and tell her. Just as I said it." The line goes dead.

I knock on the bedroom door. Mrs Schaumbacher is up in two ticks. "What is it, Margaret? Not another tummy ache?" Everyone knows about my stomach problems. It's probably the bubblegum, but maybe I've got a peptic ulcer. Maybe because I don't chew my food enough times before I swallow.

I tell Mrs Schaumbacher about the phone call and pass on the message. Funny that she doesn't ask me what it's got to do with the price of eggs. She just makes me repeat it, and doesn't even bother to pull on her dressing gown.

"I'll deal with it, Lenny," she whispers to Mr Schaumbacher, and hurries to the phone. "Back to bed, Margaret."

I don't close the bedroom door. I just stand there. The sound of dialling, then I hear her voice. "You'll pass it on to the others. Mrs Gray has taken her dog for a walk." Silence. "Yes, of course Lenny is here. Don't worry, we'll be fine." Then it's quiet again. I slip behind the door as she passes. Benny's voice comes down the passage, soft at first, and then louder. She hushes him.

A few minutes later there's hammering at the front door. It's rude and scary. Feet slowly stomp down the passage. A door opens and there's the sound of voices. Men speaking with Afrikaans accents.

"Come on, man, my family is sleeping. This is bloody harassment." Mr Schaumbacher sounds angry.

I put on my dressing gown and peep into the passage.

Benny is standing there. The scar on his lip is a white line. We walk to the front room and Benny pulls his legs up on the couch. He looks like he's been kicked in the stomach. All the lights in the house are on.

"You've already searched my home twice this year. What on earth are you looking for?" Mrs Schaumbacher comes in, followed by two men. She sucks in her breath when she sees me. "I thought I told you to go back to bed?"

Mr Schaumbacher puts his arms around her. "It's okay, darling. I'm here."

"It's not personal, Mr Schaumbacher. Please tell your wife to co-operate. Else it's going to go bad for you." The man has a big yellow handkerchief tucked into the top pocket of his suit.

Behind him is a man with a moustache. He makes me think of Oliver Hardy, the fat friend of Stan Laurel, except he doesn't have a face that makes me want to laugh. It's red, with acne scars, and the skin on his fat neck looks like Zacharias's strawberries at the end of summer.

The handkerchief man goes to the bookshelves. He starts pulling out books, tossing some onto the floor, others into a box. "Eisenhower. Sounds Russian," he says, throwing the book into the box.

Mr Schaumbacher watches them, lighting one cigarette, and then another. They just sit in the ashtray, growing long ashes.

"Why don't you and Benny play some cards until these gentlemen finish? Go on, go and sit by the bay window." Mrs

Schaumbacher shoves a box of Bicycle cards into my hands. "Please, Benny and Margaret, I want you out of the way. On the window seat. Please." She gives my bottom a pat as she shoos us to the window.

We join Charles on the window seat. Most nights, he sleeps at the Schaumbachers. I think he's adopted them.

"Who are those men?" I ask.

Benny shrugs. "The Grays. It's always the same ones."

We play Donkey. The Joker card is the Donkey. I win every time because I trick Benny into taking it. I make a big show of hiding a card in the middle of my hand, so he thinks it's the Joker. Of course, he goes and chooses the card on the side. "Donkey, Donkey, Donkey!"

Benny's mind isn't on the game. He watches the men piling papers and books into boxes and then shifting them out the door to their car. They take enough books to open a library.

The handkerchief man goes into Mr Schaumbacher's study. The other man goes off to the bedrooms. Even though there aren't any bookshelves, he's there an awful long time. Mr Schaumbacher keeps popping in and out, watching them.

They come back, and one has a shoebox in his hands. Mrs Schaumbacher reaches for the box. "Please, those are private letters. They're from my husband when we were courting."

He just laughs and starts reading in a loud voice: "I ache for you, I long to taste your lips again. Darling Rachel, you are my life, my heart." The handkerchief man also laughs. "Kinky stuff for a bunch of commies." Mrs Schaumbacher turns away and takes a tissue from the pocket of her gown.

I've seen the handkerchief man somewhere before. Then I remember and say, "Hey, Mr Gray, how's your daughter?"

He squints at me as I sit on the window seat.

"Don't you remember? My father came to your house to see to Gertie's sore tummy after pancake Tuesday. He got her to the hospital before her appendix burst." I slowly nod at him. "Yes, I was with him on that house call. I bet she's got an impressive scar?"

He rubs his forehead like he has a headache. "There's nothing else here. Let's go." They each take a box of books, and walk to the front door.

"Ag no, man, that blerrie animal sprayed all over my hat," he shouts. "Yessus, man, I'll moer that cat."

Trust Charles to embarrass me in front of guests again.

"We'll be back. And next time we're coming for you." His face looks purple as he points a finger at Mr Schaumbacher.

My stomach feels hollow. I haven't slept enough, but Mrs Schaumbacher says there's no point in going back to bed. She makes us coffee and toast with Black Cat peanut butter and golden syrup. After breakfast, I look for Nancy Drew. She's safe and sound, next to Benny's bed.

Mavis comes in, her hands on her hips. "Not as messy as last time," she says. "They didn't find anything?" Mrs Schaumbacher shakes her head.

When Moses arrives, Mr Schaumbacher gets him cracking with the leaves piled up behind the garden shed.

Mrs Schaumbacher opens the flap of the window seat and

pulls out some books and papers. She passes a pile to Benny and me and sends us off to the bonfire Moses has made outside. At first I feel sinful about throwing books into the fire, but Mrs Schaumbacher says it has to be done.

I chuck them onto the flames, trying to grab more than Benny. *Fighting Talk.* Yes, that should burn. *Zambia Shall Be Free.* Who's Zambia and why's he in jail, I wonder, but then I stop reading the titles when I see Benny's beating me. Moses uses a garden fork, stabbing them as they land in the fire. I tell Benny it's like Guy Fawkes. Remember, remember, the fifth of November. But it's a bit early, and we don't have marshmallows or sparklers.

Mrs Schaumbacher stands close by, making sure that not a bit of paper is left when the fire dies down. She gets all teared up. I suppose the smoke got in her eyes.

Gemima wraps a towel around my shoulders and presses my head down, wetting my hair in the basin.

"Ag no, man, Mima. This water is cold." I try to lift my head but her hand pushes against the back of my neck.

"It wasn't cold when I called you twenty minutes ago." Gemima puts a blob of Sunsilk on her palm and rubs it on my hair. "No. Just keep your head down. Next time don't stand so close to the fire. Your mummy doesn't like your hair smelling all smoky."

After rinsing the shampoo off, she takes the plug out. She fills a jug of clean water from the bath. "One more rinse and it's over for the week."

It's far from over, though. After rubbing my hair with a towel, Gemima goes at it with the comb, pulling at a knot. "If you would just keep it short we wouldn't have this problem."

I'm never cutting my hair again. It was only when I turned seven that my mother let me grow my hair. It always looked like someone had put a potty on my head and chopped around it with a pair of garden shears.

"But your hair is so fine. If you keep it short you'll have lovely thick hair like Lucy in a couple of years," my mother said. She fibbed. My hair is still thin and fine. Lucy calls it bum-fluff. At least it's long enough to wear a pony now.

"Go outside. It'll soon be dry, the sun is lovely today." Gemima hangs the towel on the rail.

I sit in the sun with the Hardy Boys, watching the road. The green Volksie opposite the Schaumbachers is there again. I wave at it. Sometimes it drives away after dropping off an African. He just stands there on the pavement, staring at the house all day. I asked my father about it one morning and he said, "Ignore them. They're just playing a silly game with the Schaumbachers."

It doesn't look like a fun game to play, nothing ever happens. When we had a freak rainstorm last month, the African wore plastic with a hole cut in the top. Just his head stuck out. I bet he still got sopping wet.

The MacPhail's truck is parked in the road and I see the coal boy with his sooty sack over his hair. He runs through the service entrance, carrying our monthly delivery on his head. The mielie lady runs too, shouting "Meee-Leees!" The basket on her head drops some cobs as the Dobermann puppy from number 29 yaps at her heels. I yell, "Bad dog, bad dog," but it doesn't listen.

I spy Sophie across the road getting the week's fruit and vegetables from the sammy. He drives off down the road in his green panel van. In a few minutes, the butcher's boy will arrive on his bicycle, the wicker basket in front packed with our meat order.

Roger the Dodger's car comes screaming around the corner. Lucy's driving, though she shouldn't. She's only just got her licence. She jerks to a stop in the driveway, right by the front of the house. She flicks a cigarette butt out of the window and calls to me.

"Hey, brat, can you do me a favour?" Lucy makes it seem like she's the one doing something for me, when it's actually the other way around. I don't mind. After doing the favour, she sometimes lets me brush her hair and fold her nylons. Then she says, "Fine, you can voetsek now."

I help Lucy carry two boxes out of the car. I tell her: "You can put them in my hospital if you like?" The hospital is in the spare room where I keep my sick dolls. Every one of my dolls is sick. They aren't much use to me unless they need medical attention.

"No, put them outside in the ironing room. I want them out of the way. You take this one, it's lighter. I can manage the other." Lucy struggles with her box.

"What's in them?"

Lucy's hair covers her face as she plonks the box down. "Just some of Roger's law books. He's gone away and I said I'd keep them for him."

"Where's he gone? Doesn't he need his books for studying?"

Lucy has her back to me and doesn't answer.

JENNA

Aunt C-C is standing by the gate when I arrive on Monday afternoon, almost exactly where I'd left her three days before, as though she'd planted herself on the pavement and grown roots. She's talking to the security guy, the one who treated me like a wannabe burglar and wrote me up in his notebook.

I stand back and listen, curious to find out what's going on. The guards always know whose dog's gone missing, who got hijacked in their driveway, and who's been dumping their rubbish in the park at the end of the street, causing the other residents to post angry messages on the Facebook community page. Because trash doesn't clean itself, you know, and the municipality ain't gonna bother.

The two of them are waist-high in Zulu and speaking so fast I can't catch a word. My Zulu is pretty non-existent. I got as far as greeting and introducing myself in Grade Three, and then decided to chuck it in. *Sawubona, igama lami nguJenna.* That's about it.

Virgins also offers Afrikaans as a second language for matric. *Goeie middag, my naam is Jenna.* I'm also rubbish at Afrikaans. If you need directions out of Pofadder, or want to order a boerewors roll at a kerkbasaar, please don't bother to ask me. You're on your own.

Her jaw set, Aunt C-C says to the guard: "I'll see what I can do, Clever. I'll let you know." She taps him on the shoulder, then turns and hustles me through the gate, slamming it shut behind us. I follow her down the pathway, jacaranda pods cracking under my shoes.

She shambles towards the front door, muttering in Zulu and spewing clicks. She makes a sudden switch to English. "I just can't stand these people. They think they're living twenty years ago. When will they realise they can't carry on behaving like this?" She pushes open the door and stands in the hallway. She's panting like a little dog and her eyes are about to pop.

I reach across and place a hand under her elbow. "Can I get you something? Maybe you should sit down?"

She slaps me away. "Don't speak to me like I'm some useless old woman. I'm perfectly capable, you know."

I don't think I can take her word for it. She fumbles along the passage wall, leaning against it until her breathing steadies. "The arrogance, the greed. I just can't bear it."

I'm not keen to stand here watching her talk to the wall all day. I've got things to do. "Can I have a drink of water? It's really hot, and I'm feeling a bit thirsty."

"The kitchen's just there, you'll find a bottle in the fridge. It's from a tap. Johannesburg water is the best in the world, you know. I won't tolerate the rubbish you can buy in the shops."

I don't bother with the fridge, my hands go straight to the

kitchen drawers. Come on, where is it? Something that'll tell me more about Holly's letter to her. About Danny. Anything.

My fingers find a book under a mess of stationery, elastic bands and keys. It's an old exercise book covered in brown paper and plastic, the kind a kid would use at school. Stuck onto the front is a Christmas card with a robin in a tree, and above it, in childish handwriting, the words *Gemima's Special Book.*

I flip through the pages. It's filled with cuttings from a newspaper, each one headed: *Ann Wise Replies.*

I turn back to the first page. Surrounded by a gold border drawn with pencil crayon is a single newspaper cutting:

This week I received a marvellously useful tip from Gemima, who has worked in Johannesburg for the Channing-Court family for nearly twenty years. Have any of our housewives ever despaired over those hard bits of bathroom soap? Well, don't throw them away. Gemima's tip is most economical and proves extremely useful in getting your laundry whiter than white. Your madam is lucky indeed to have you, Gemima!

I don't get a chance to read Gemima's useful tip, Holly will just have to carry on tossing the bits of soap and settle for grey undies. Aunt C-C wanders into the kitchen, so I shove the book back in.

I open the fridge and reach for the lonely bottle of water. It's clear that Aunt C-C and Holly have the same enthusiasm for shopping. Hey, there's no place like home, Toto.

"So, what did Clever do to upset you?" I hold the bottle to my lips, but Aunt C-C grimaces and I put it down without so much as a sip. She reaches for a glass, hands it to me. She sets a cup and saucer on a tray, and places a beaded doily over a milk jug.

She doesn't answer, so I give it another go. "The security guard, I think you called him Clever? What's he done to make you so cross?"

Aunt C-C's face twitches. "Don't be foolish, girl. You heard us. His employers have told him he's lost his job and he must go back to Zimbabwe. Not only is it illegal, it's downright inhuman." She swirls water around in the teapot, empties it in the sink, spoons in some Earl Grey leaves, and fills it with water again. She puts a tea cosy over it and repeats: "You were there, you heard us."

"I didn't get it. I don't speak Zulu."

Her face twitches again. "Oh, for goodness' sake, don't tell me you're one of those people who lives in this country and hasn't bothered to learn an African language. How on earth do you communicate?"

Oh, get a life. Everyone speaks English these days. It's called globalisation, Aunt Know-it-all. I go for the appeasement option. "A lot of whiteys still haven't changed, you know. Those employers are racists, I suppose."

"I didn't say they were white. You shouldn't make assumptions, Jenny, it's ignorant." Her eyes are hard, daring me to hit her so she can punch me back. Challenge accepted.

"My name isn't Jenny. I've told you, it's Jenna." Fine, I wimped out. I'm not into having a boring discussion about race with this dinosaur. She's as bad as Xoliswa.

"Indeed. Your mother's parents were also a bit silly when it came to names. Holly! How ridiculous!" She raises a wispy eyebrow. "I believe your grandfather was mad for Audrey Hepburn and *Breakfast at Tiffany's*. What's wrong with Heloise, I ask you? Now *there's* a good family name."

Aunt C-C swats at a fly on the Formica tabletop. "I'd like you to clear one of the bedrooms today. I have someone coming from the orphanage at the end of the week so I need it all packed up." Ignoring my offer of help, she carries the tray upstairs. "This was the spare room when my family lived here. Not that we had many visitors." She pushes open the door and smiles. "Sometimes it was used as a hospital for dolls."

"Was this my mom's room?" Four crappy years Holly spent here, she says. She got the hell out, or was thrown out when she fell pregnant. After Danny murdered someone, or someone murdered Danny – who may or may not be my father.

I'd long ago accepted that some young guy had decided having a kid before he was out of his teens was a double negative. People were allowed to make these sorts of informed decisions. It's a free world, right? But he wasn't informed. If he knew about me, I know he'd want me. If he's alive.

Aunt C-C ignores my question. "Clothes, toys and books in separate boxes," she instructs me. "There's nothing else in here, I think. It's been used as something of a dumping place."

It sure is a trash heap. Piles of books litter the narrow bed, and through gaping wardrobe doors I see a mangle of toys:

dirty-pink legs and dull gold hair among a pile of clothes.

"I need to make a few telephone calls. Get on with it and don't forget to label the boxes."

The door clicks shut. What the heck should I tackle first? Clothes. I take each item, shake it out, and fold it into a box. I'm used to rummaging through clothes at the Hospice shop with Holly. She's an old-clothes freak. "Look, Jenna, a dress from the sixties. Vintage! What a score! They'll look awesome with the cowboy boots I found last week." She'd have gone crazy in here. Shame for Holly the clothes were made for someone half her size.

Everything is last-century and handmade, even the red-and-white checked school dresses. They're Virgins issue, in great nick. The seams are straight, the hems hand-stitched in tiny diagonals. I could do with a new uniform. Holly gets mine from the school's clothing exchange.

I fill three boxes, working fast, desperate to get onto something that will tell me more about Holly's time here. I tackle the books, hold each one up by the spine as I shake the pages, willing something to fall out. The Secret Seven, Nancy Drew and the Hardy Boys – they all warn: *This book belongs to Margaret Beatrice Channing-Court.* A few illustrated stories from the Bible: Noah leading the animals into the ark, Moses in a wicker basket among the bulrushes, and David, sling in hand, about to slay Goliath.

There's nothing here. The lounge is where I need to be. There's still the rest of the stuff in the chest of drawers, I could check it out.

I push open the bedroom door and peer along the passage. Aunt C-C's got her back to me, the phone stuck to her ear. "Don't you dare call me an interfering umlungu. Yes, I'm white but I know what that means. Throwing that race nonsense around doesn't intimidate me."

I edge down the passage towards the stairs as her voice hammers on. "I don't care that he is illegal, the labour laws in this country still apply." She slams down the phone. Eish, the woman's hectic! I almost feel sorry for Clever's boss.

In the lounge, the boxes are where I'd left them on Friday. But something has changed. The bookshelf is bare, the photo albums are gone. I reach into the bottom drawer. It's empty.

At the sound of coughing, I glance up. Aunt C-C is staring at me. "Are you looking for something in here? I thought I asked you to pack up the spare room?"

"The Koki pen," I mutter. "To mark the boxes." I spot it lying on the floor next to some bubble wrap, pick it up, and leave the lounge. I hurry upstairs, Aunt C-C following slowly behind me.

The toys in the wardrobe stare at me with plastic orbs, their eyelashes long and spiky. They give me the creeps. I look under the bed. Boxes. This is more like it. The first, a shoebox, the lid stabbed with holes, is full of moth carcases and empty cocoons. Gross! I put the lid back on and shove it under the bed. A biscuit tin is filled with old sewing patterns. And there's a stack of comics in a big cardboard box. *Superman, Beano, Archie and Jughead.* At the bottom, a white book with gold-edged pages. I open it, read the inscription:

Elizabeth Heloise Fitzmaurice, 1933. From her Mother, on her First Holy Communion. Folded inside is a newspaper article – and also a letter. At last!

Spidery writing in faded blue ink fills the flimsy pages.

> *12 Stafford Terrace,*
> *Kensington W8,*
> *London.*
> *6 August 1963.*

Dearest Ellie,

Thank you for your letter which I received yesterday. I am pleased that Margaret liked the books we sent. Little Lord Fauntleroy *is, as you know, a particular favourite of mine and I just knew she would adore it too.*

I am sorry that Mother's letter has upset you, but she is still in an awful sulk about the Forresters. Miss Forrester has been perfectly horrid about it all, going around town saying that your children have gone native. Did Lucy really quote Karl Marx to Bishop Forrester? I so wish I had been there to see his face, he's such a stuffed shirt. What a giggle!

It will, of course, blow over, kitten. As for me, you know I don't give a monkey's if you allow Margaret to play with the sons of Jews or communists, I have become quite the liberal in my old age. And Lucy is a darling, headstrong as she is. If she chooses to wear dresses the size of a handkerchief, bully for her. (If

Albert would allow it, I'd let my Gilly and Babs do the same.)

I am, however, a little concerned, so bear with your over-solicitous older sister. I have enclosed a clipping from The Times. *A tad worrying, I'm sure you'll agree? That wretched government of yours seems awfully gung-ho, being as beastly as possible with their new security laws, scooping up communists and agitators willy-nilly, and keeping them locked up for months ahead of that tedious Mandela trial of theirs.*

So, dearest, it might be wise to place a little distance between yourself and your neighbours. I know that you and Rachel Schaumbacher have always been on the friendliest of terms, but I would so hate to see you and David hurt by the association. Be kind, but firm. Remember, darling, family comes first.

I'm afraid I have to end this letter to catch the post. Before I run off, though, a final word about Mother being so horrid to you: perhaps the straw that broke the camel's back wasn't so much Charles powdering his whiskers on the pouf, but having jelly in the trifle. Poor Mother will never live that down (I, of course, refuse to believe you would be so vulgar!). Darling, take care of yourself, I do so worry about your nerves. Chin up!

Your loving sister,
Beatrice

As I put the letter back into the envelope I read the newspaper headline: *Hundreds held in police swoop.* The newsprint is so tiny that I don't bother with the rest.

I return the book to the box, and as I pack the comics on top, just as I'd found them, I spot a school yearbook sticking out from the pile – and I recognise Virgins' crest.

The yearbook pages are always crammed with the girls' proudest moments. Photographs of the first hockey team, the debating team, the swots in their blazers for academic colours. To say that I don't feature prominently in my yearbook is an understatement. The date on this one is the year Holly left school. 2001. She was also at Virgins, like Aunt C-C. It's a Channing-Court tradition. I could never crack a bursary, and I haven't a clue how Holly manages the fees.

I page through the book. No sign of Holly. I guess we have something in common. I get near the end to the Matric Dance. This is one thing Holly would never have given a miss, being a party girl. There she is. Sheesh, Holly, where on earth did you get that dress! She wouldn't be seen dead in something like this today. Her partner is stuffed into a white suit, and it's as if he's in a straitjacket. But there's nothing uptight about their smiles. *Holly Moore and her Danny-boy!*

My finger hovers over the face in the photograph. His hair is dark and curly, and he's tall – like me. I rip the page out of the yearbook and put it into my pocket.

"Did you find anything interesting?" Aunt C-C's crept up on me.

"Some old comics. Do you want me to put them in the

box with the other books? They're collectables, you know, worth a fortune on eBay."

"Comics? No, we were never allowed to read those as children. Perhaps they belonged to your mother."

"They're really old. But I'll ask her."

"Well, *do* ask her why she hasn't bothered to return my phone call. I've put together a few of her possessions and I would like her to come and fetch them."

"I can take them when I leave. No prob."

"No, tell her she must come for her things." She pauses and says, "No prob."

Slap me, the old witch actually smiled.

I pull the toys out of the wardrobe. Yellow and purple paint bruise the pink limbs, and the stomachs are blotched with red. One doll is missing a leg, another has a hole gouged into its foot. Seriously vicious.

A life-size baby doll with a dummy in its mouth is wrapped in an old nappy, as if it were a shroud. It's like something out of a bad psycho movie. The person who owned these dolls was a sicko.

I toss the toys into boxes, my skin crawling.

MARGARET

The yowling outside my window wakes me. Charles. It sounds like he's in ghastly pain. I slide my feet down into the coldness of my sheets, searching for the hot-water bottle. My toes touch it. Lukewarm.

The howling carries on. I put on my dressing gown and slippers and tiptoe downstairs, through the kitchen and out the back door. With its annoying creak, I don't risk shutting it.

"Sssk-sssk-sssk. Hey, kitty." The light from the three-quarter moon makes shadows in the garden. The Milky Way follows stars that look like they've been flung against the black sky like confetti. "Sssk-sssk-sssk."

I hear rustling near the tyre-swing tree and look up. Charles mewls pitifully, his eyes glowing in the bare branches. My gown blows open and I feel an icy wind through my flannel pyjamas.

"Are you stuck?" I say. "You foolish cat. You're too old to climb trees."

Lucy says cats can't get stuck in trees. Like fish drowning in water, it can't happen. If I leave him, he'll make his own way down in his own good time. From deep inside his bladder, Charles gives an almighty squall.

"Stop howling, Charles, you're getting on my nerves." A whisp of my breath floats in front of me.

"Margaret, is that you?"

I nearly jump out of my skin. Cats can't talk.

"Margaret. Over here." My eyes search the garden. I spot a long dark shadow on the grass and move towards it. I recognise the bearded face and black hair and give a croaky laugh.

"Jislaaik, Mr Schaumbacher, I got such a fright. Why are you on the lawn? It's jolly cold out here. You'll catch your death."

"Please, keep your voice down a bit there, Margaret. If you could just lend me a hand. I'm finding it hard to walk."

I stretch out my hand and he slowly gets up. He groans, wobbling as he grips my arm. "I think I've twisted this ankle of mine. Do you mind if I …?" He puts an arm around my shoulder. I feel myself sagging and he's down on the grass again. Toppling over.

"Let me call my father. Or Mrs Schaumbacher?" The lights next door are like the Tower of Light at the Rand Easter Show. Shadows move behind the net curtains. Benny's up very early this morning.

"No, no, please, Margaret. You mustn't go next door. If you could just call your dad I'd be most grateful." He sighs and stretches out on the grass, his face white in the moonlight. "Just try to be quiet about it, please."

I make my way back into the house and creep upstairs to

my parents' bedroom. I glance down at my mother, curled on her side, her eyes covered by a sleeping mask, her skin shiny with Pond's. As I reach the bed near the window, my father raises his head. "Everything all right, Mags? You want some Milk of Magnesia for your tummy?" He's whispering, careful not to wake my mother.

"I need you, Daddy. Come quick."

My father puts on his slippers and ties the cord around his gown. After a glance at the other bed, he follows me out and shuts the door.

I place a finger against my lips, take his hand, and lead him downstairs to the kitchen. "It's Mr Schaumbacher. I found him in our garden and he can't walk."

My father doesn't ask any questions. He follows me out of the back door without a word. A warm body brushes against my ankles – it's Charles, making a dash into the kitchen. We carry on, me in front, past the tyre-swing tree to where I'd left Mr Schaumbacher.

"Terribly sorry to get you out of bed at this ungodly hour, Doc. I'm afraid I'm in a spot of bother. It's my ankle. I can't walk."

"Let's get you indoors." My father helps him to his feet, and with Mr Schaumbacher's arm across his shoulders, they limp towards the house and into the kitchen. "Through here, into the front room, it'll be warmer."

Mr Schaumbacher grabs my father's hand as he fumbles for the light switch. "No, not the light. It'll be visible from the road. Please, it's too dangerous."

The coals in the fire from last night are white, but still

EDYTH BULBRING

warm. My father lowers Mr Schaumbacher into a leather chair. "Hand me a torch, Mags. It's in the drawer of your mother's writing desk." I pass it to him and his fingers cover the beam. "Let me take a look at that ankle of yours."

Mr Schaumbacher stretches his leg out on the ottoman. He's barefoot, and the edges of his pyjama trousers are covered in yellow grass. My father gives me the torch. "Point it over here, Mags. No, don't wave it all over the room."

"Is it the ligaments? Perhaps the anterior talofibular ligament? Or maybe it's broken? Don't forget to palpate the fibula. Can I do it? Please, Daddy?"

"Stop jumping up and down, Mags, I need to see what I'm doing."

Mr Schaumbacher moans as my father feels his ankle. "It's not broken, Lenny, but it's a bad sprain. A couple of bags of frozen peas should bring down the swelling. I'll bandage it later and it should be fine in a few days. But you'll have to keep the pressure off it for a while."

My father sends me to the kitchen for frozen peas. When I come back, I stop outside the door.

"I'm sorry to involve you like this, Doc. They came for me at about three this morning. I got away by the skin of my teeth. If they'd found me and held me under ninety days, I doubt they'd let me out again."

"You know I have no truck with your politics, Lenny, but these people are just not playing the game any more. They've gone beyond all that is decent. Are Rachel and Benny going to be all right?"

"They've never had reason to cause trouble with Rachel. She's kept herself well out of my activities. I expect they're still there turning the house upside down, just to aggravate the situation. If I could just stay here for a couple of hours until I'm sure they're gone, I'll be on my way."

"Where will you go?"

"I'll have to lie low for a few weeks until arrangements can be made. Living in this country isn't an option any more. They've tied me up tighter than a Christmas turkey with their ruddy laws."

I step into the room and hand my father the packets of frozen peas. He places one below and another on top of Mr Schaumbacher's ankle.

I take the torch and snuggle up with the Famous Five close to the fire, but my father say's I'll ruin my eyes. So we sit in silence for a while, listening to the sounds of the morning.

Dogs bark as the dustbin boys shout and bang the heavy metal bins, emptying the rubbish into the truck. When they bring the bins back, they slam the lids down. The truck drives off, and they whistle and call out, running behind it.

The milk van rumbles up and the milk boy runs to our door, the bottles clinking. He'll take the tokens Gemima left with the empties. There's a thump as the newspaper hits the gravel in the driveway and the paper boy cycles on. As the dawn flickers on the walls, the back door creaks. Mr Schaumbacher sits up.

"It's just Ntombi come to light the stove." My father removes the soggy bags of peas and dries Mr Schaumbacher's ankle with a handkerchief. He takes out a bandage and some metal clips. "I think we should move you before it's completely light. I'll get you some things. We can't have you running around town in your pyjamas."

Mr Schaumbacher and I are left alone with the defrosted peas. I know what we're having for supper tonight.

"Would you mind lending me some paper and a pen, Margaret?"

I search through my mother's writing desk and tear a page from an old prescription pad. I hand it to Mr Schaumbacher together with a pencil stub. He writes with quick strokes, folds the paper, and passes it to me. "You'll ask Benny to give this to his mom. It's important. He mustn't show it to anyone else."

I tuck it into my dressing-gown pocket. "I promise I'll give it to Benny." I don't tell Mr Schaumbacher I promise not to read it. Benny's always sneaking looks at my letters, so fair's fair.

My father walks in. He's wearing a pullover and casual trousers and has some extra clothes in his arms. We wait in the kitchen as Mr Schaumbacher dresses. Gemima fills the kettle. "Will the other master be eating breakfast, Doctor?"

"I think it'd be best if he and I left now. And, Ntombi, no porridge for me this morning. I'll have coffee and eggs when I get back."

I watch them get into my father's Chevy. Mr Schaumbacher lies down in the back, and they drive off. I wanted to go with them but my father said no, I needed to be home in case my mother wanted something. "Don't bother her with all of this. It can be between you and me, Mags. Just tell her it was a medical emergency if she asks. I won't be long."

Mr Schaumbacher winked at me when he said goodbye. I winked back. His note was safe with me.

I drag my school shoes along the pavement, scuffing the toes. I leave Gemima at the front gate and wander over to Benny's. He wasn't at school today, and the note his father gave me is burning a hole in my blazer pocket.

Benny's hiding in our hollowed-out den in the privet hedge. It's our Secret Seven den. And sometimes it's our secret bunker for when the Russians come. Miss van Tonder told us they're waiting in their submarines off the coast of Port St Johns, and it's only a matter of time before they invade our country and let the garden boys swim in our swimming pools and marry our sisters. I know Lucy's safe, though, because Zacharias is already married. But still, Benny and I take precautions.

There are dark rings around Benny's eyes. He either has an iron deficiency, or he slept badly. The symptoms are similar. I offer him his father's note and he smacks my hand away. "What's this? Another piece of blank paper from that stupid pen pal of yours?"

"Your father was at our house last night and he asked me to give it to you."

Benny lifts his lip.

"If you don't want it, that's just fine with me." I pretend to rip it up.

"Don't. Just give it here. You're not funny." He snatches the note and ducks away without even saying thank you. He stops, then runs screaming into the house. "Mom! Where are you? Mom."

I follow Benny inside, wiping leaves from my hair. I almost trip over Charles, who's sunning himself on the kitchen floor. Mavis is fond of him and lets him visit when Gemima shoos him out.

Mrs Schaumbacher is busy at her Singer, pedalling as if her life depended on it. Bits of a Simplicity pattern are spread out on the floor. The wireless is playing "Blame It On The Bossa Nova". It's by Eydie Gormé, and is one of Lucy's favourites.

Benny turns up the radio and hands her the note. His mouth opens and closes, but I can't really hear what he's saying. Mrs Schaumbacher unfolds the page and smooths it out on her lap.

After reading it this morning, I'd folded it along the old creases. There's no way she'd know. The message was nothing to shout home about: *Phone your favourite cousin and ask him for the telephone number of the person whose wife did the flowers for your nephew's bar mitzvah. My love always.*

Mrs Schaumbacher gets up, strikes a match and holds the note above an ashtray. We all watch it burn away, and then she turns to me. "Do you think I might use your telephone, Margaret? Ours isn't reliable."

Benny's phone never works as it should. It crackles and hisses and Benny says his mother doesn't like to chat too long. They're forever using ours or the tickey box on the corner.

I take Mrs Schaumbacher home with me, and while she's on the phone I go upstairs to tell my mother that Mrs Schaumbacher is paying a visit. My mother is up and dressed. She's listening to *Women's World* while she tacks the hem of my school uniform. She says she can't see Mrs Schaumbacher and I am not to tell Gemima to offer her tea. After making her call, Mrs Schaumbacher hurries home to Benny.

Back in my hospital, I'm sawing away at Cindy's gangrenous ankle when my mother walks in. She's wringing her hands. "It's ridiculous. How can the girl get into Lucy's room to clean it if it's always locked?" She runs a hand through her hair. "What's got into that child? Locking doors, as if this house is some kind of penitentiary."

I leave Cindy in the middle of her amputation and follow my mother downstairs. She's calling for Lucy. "Lucy! Loo-cy!" Her voice rises. "Looo-cy." I join her. "Looo-cy."

Gemima's in the passageway. "I'll find her for you, Madam."

As my mother walks off, Gemima catches me by the ear. "Go get your sister. She's outside in the ironing room."

I find Lucy ironing a grubby shirt.

"Aren't you supposed to wash shirts before you iron them?"

Lucy jumps. "Yirre, brat. You scared me to death."

"What you doing, Luce? That's Mima's job. She'll kill you

if you break her iron." I look down at the shirt. "That's not one of Daddy's shirts. Mima's got a special trick to make them extra-white. And you're doing it wrong. Mima uses starch when she irons. Wait till Mummy hears what you're doing. She's already cross about you locking your bedroom." I shift away from the door.

"Wait." Lucy puts down the iron, gathers the shirt in her hands. "Please don't say anything. If I tell you, promise you won't split on me, and I'll give you a special present."

I'm dying to know, but I give her my bored face. Then I lick a finger and say, "Cross my heart and hope to die. Your secret is safe with me for ever and ever and ever …"

"That's enough for evers. But seriously, hand on Bible, Mags." She gives me a stern look. "If you break this promise, you know you'll go to hell?"

"I don't need a Bible. I promised on my heart."

"It's Roger's shirt. I've been doing his washing. I do it every day."

"Doesn't he have his own maid to wash his clothes?"

"Roger's staying at Marshall Square for a while. You know, it's that red-brick building in Main Street. He's on a special holiday from the university and there aren't any maids to cook and do his washing. So I take him food and a fresh set of clothes every day."

"But you can't cook. Poor Roger, he must be starving."

"Mima's been helping me with that. She also washes and irons the clothes – but only after I've finished with them. Mummy mustn't know. Or Daddy. You know they think

Roger's a useless layabout. They'll have a fit if they found out."

"What do you mean, finished with them? Why were you ironing his dirty shirt?" It hits me with the force of one of Benny's punches on my arm. "Secret messages! Am I right? Am I? Oh tell me, Lucy, please!"

She holds the shirt out to me. There's some yellowish writing on the collar.

"Is that lemon juice?"

"I hope so. I send him a lemon every day. At first he used his wee."

"Sis! He didn't, did he? He must've been desperate."

"I swear to God, Mags, you tell on me and I'll wring your neck."

I glance at the two boxes in the corner of the room. "You're still keeping Roger's university books. Shouldn't you take them to him so he can study while he's on holiday?"

"They're a secret too, Mags. Daddy and Mummy can't know. But I'm going to move them out of here soon. Don't say anything about any of this. The boxes or the shirts. Promise?"

I lick my finger again and cross my heart.

When I go to bed I find Lucy's autograph book under my pillow. A present for me. She's got dozens of autographs from famous people: Cliff Richard, Margot Fonteyn – and best of all, three Miss South Africas. She hasn't got my favourite, Yvonne Ficker, because she stopped collecting autographs a couple of years ago. I read the clever messages from her friends. One is from a boy called Brian Unsworth:

Tulips in the garden
Tulips in the park
But the best tulips
Are two lips in the dark.

I tuck the autograph book under my pillow and switch off the light. I'll keep my promise to Lucy. I won't say a word to anyone, not even to Benny.

The next afternoon, Lucy drives away in Roger the Dodger's car to Marshall Square with a set of clean clothes and a basket of food. A roast chicken and some naartjies are wrapped in yesterday's *Star* because Lucy says Roger needs something to read apart from the Bible.

JENNA

I pull the duvet off Holly and try to drag her out of bed. She's alone, for once. Barry must have left sometime in the night.

"It's not raining, do I have to?" She falls back, holding the duvet up to her chin, refusing to budge.

"It's camp. I need a lift with my gear. I can't lug it all to school." I jerk the duvet and there's a tussle as she yanks it back. "If I'm not there by seven they'll leave without me. Come on, Holly, give me a break."

She stretches, tosses the sheet aside. Argh, no pyjamas. She's in great shape for an old person. Her body is brown with no tan marks. No stretch marks, either. No wonder Barry was so surprised when he met me last night.

He gets a one-and-a-half rating on the boyfriend scale. I could push it to two, but his chinos are too tight around his bum and he speaks in capital letters. "Good GOD, woman. She's a mini YOU. Who'd have THOUGHT you had a TEENAGE daughter?"

Holly obviously hadn't told him about me. It's like I'm some dirty little secret. I suppose lots of men run a mile at this kind of baggage. Still, it's a pity her commitment to upfront honesty doesn't extend past her sales technique.

I make her a strong cup of coffee while she gets dressed. Seriously, I'll kill her if I miss the bus.

"Where's that camp list, I know I put it somewhere?" Holly swallows a yawn, pulling a sweatshirt over her head. "I suppose you'll need padkos. Is there any bread?"

"I'm sorted. And I don't need sandwiches for the road. We're only going to the Magaliesberg."

I glance at the clock on the wall. Relax, Jenna, there's time.

"They used to take us to Zinkwazi in KZN. You know my Grandpa Frank had a farm somewhere there yonks ago. It was amazing. He sold it a few years after I was born. Too old to manage it. I suppose if my mother had given him a grandson he might have held on." She stirs her coffee and puts the wet spoon back into the sugar bowl. Makes me want to slap her.

"Who's Danny?" I say.

She steps back as if I'd punched her, then carries on. "Ja, Zinkwazi. I'm sure that's where we went when I was at Virgins. Just swimming and surfing – a *real* school camp."

"I don't care about your camp. I want to know about Danny." I shove the page from the yearbook in her face, my finger stabbing at the photo. "Who's your Danny-boy?"

Holly takes the page and gives a shaky laugh. "Oh, this old photo. Where'd you find it? Wowza, check out my dress! Fashion crime, hey?"

"Stop it. I'm sick of your lies. I want to know about him." I pull the page out of her hand. "I found it in the school library." Fine, I'm a liar too.

Holly lowers herself onto a chair and rubs her eyes. "He

was an old boyfriend of mine."

"Yes, when you were in matric. You went to the dance together." I stand in front of her, my arms folded, demanding answers. "Is he my father?"

Holly holds out her hands, palms up. "Jenna, he was bad news. He was wild, totally messed up. He was into a lot of crap, drugging and drinking, and you know. He messed me up badly too. Seriously, when I was with Danny, I was totally off the rails."

I knew Holly was wild at school, at university too. She never hid this from me. We'd had the drinking-and-drugs conversation years ago, long before I discovered that drugs were something dumb people did for fun. "Listen up, Jenna, if you have to take drugs, do weed. It's a herb, part of our cultural heritage. Don't ever touch tablets or needles. And if you drink more than two, take a taxi – just don't call me." I still think she's way off-course on weed. Some girls at Virgins have done serious damage to their brains smoking the doobie.

"Baby, I just can't talk about Danny right now. It's hectic for me and it's a long story. But I promise, when you get back from camp, I'll tell you everything."

Trusting Holly is no longer an option for me. I need to know this now. "Were you still dating him when you got pregnant at university? Like, you know, dating exclusively?" I pick up my suitcase, grab the sleeping bag, and look at her. "Well, were you?"

She reaches for the car keys and nods. It tells me everything I need to know.

I slam the front door and get into the car. Holly's going to have to come clean with me. I want to know about him. As soon as I get home. And then I'll find Danny. She can't stop me.

Holly drives like a lunatic, almost hitting the car in front of us at the traffic light. She brakes hard. I look up, my heart giving a jolt. A white-painted face stares at me. A mime artist, hustling. I stare back, waiting for him to twitch or blink. Come on, blink.

There's a smashing sound in front of us. I blink. A scream, and blaring hooters.

Holly locks her door and revs as a man holding a handbag sprints off and disappears. Mr Mime pulls down the corners of his mouth, grins, and darts away.

Cars hoot. The lights are green and we drive off, the crackling of glass under our tyres. Holly doesn't say a word all the way to school. She parks close to the bus and hugs me. "Just remember, baby. I love you." I don't hug her back.

I wait around, watching as the driver loads our stuff into the side of the bus.

"Good morning, you all ready for camp?" Andile smiles at me and hands his backpack to the driver. His sleeping bag is rolled up tight at the top. Just one piece of luggage. He camps light.

"I'm dreading the ride," I say. "I get a bit queasy on these buses. Wish I could sit up front, near the driver."

"Why don't you take my place, Jen, I'll sit at the back with the rest of the sardines."

Wait, did I hear that correctly? Sucking my lip, I follow him up the stairs.

The hour-long trip into the countryside takes forever. I listen to the laughter at the back of the bus as music pumps through the speakers. "Hayibo, Xoliswa! I can't believe you know those crazy moves." Andile's voice. He's forgotten about me. Damn Xoliswa. She knows Andile's mine.

We eventually pile out and the camp counsellors show us to our cabins, warning us about the septic tanks. I take the bunk bed above Soo Ling. Her BMI is way over thirty and I don't want her falling on top of me. We're ten girls to a dormitory with one bathroom to share. Camp is no place for sissies.

"I'd like you all to split into groups of five. Today's programme involves team-building and trust exercises. Got it?" The counsellor repeats this: team building and trust. In case we forget, we each get a T-shirt: *Team Builder of the Future. Trust Me.*

We spend the afternoon leopard crawling through a maze of tunnels. Tebogo is our team leader, and we need to trust that she'll take us safely through to the other side. In record time, too, beating the other teams.

"Jeez, Xoliswa, you're kicking sand in my eyes. Go faster," I yell. She stops dead, her foot connecting with my face. "Xoliswa, just move it, dude. You're wasting time. And tell Dikeledi I know it was her that farted. I'm suffocating down here."

We're in the tunnel for what seems like hours. Soo Ling

finally loses it with Tebogo: "I thought you said your family were miners! Get a grip, retardo."

Tebogo screams from the front, her voice echoing down the tunnel. "Pee off, biiitch. My father's on the Anglo board."

"Yeah, Tebogo's family are BEE gold diggers, not stinking miners," Xoliswa shouts and kicks up more sand. I grab her ankle and give it a twist.

We finally emerge, filthy and hot, coming stone last. We're ready to rip each other's eyes out. Hooray for trust and team-building!

All ten of us rush the bathroom – there's just one shower. Zukiswa is first, of course, and uses all the hot water. Tebogo gets her back by dumping a binful of used tampons in her sleeping bag. Argh! Zukiswa's on another team, so it's all part of trust-building.

Supper is another test for the team builders of the future. Dikeledi and Soo Ling are cooking over the fire. "Look here, my friend," says Dikeledi. "This is pasta. It's not dog. You're not in Chinatown cooking for the family restaurant."

Soo Ling throws a knife at Dikeledi's feet. "Screw you, dickhead." Soo Ling is super-sensitive about her Asian heritage. Last year when some joker stuck an article about the Feast of Dogs onto her locker door, her dad raised kung-fu with the headmaster.

Andile arrives on the scene. "Hey, this looks like fun." He's spent the afternoon playing Scrabble with our biology teacher, Mrs Thomas. She's got varicose veins and wrinkles, so I don't mind too much. He tells us he got thrashed with "xenophobia". Triple letter score.

"You coming out with us tonight, sir? Not taking it easy around the fire with Mrs Thomas and a bag of marshmallows?" Xoliswa's being cute again. Doesn't she realise how pathetic she sounds?

"Are you kidding me? I'd never miss out on stalk the lantern. You guys won't get within a mile of me."

I smile in the flickering light. That's what he thinks.

After dumping Soo Ling's gluey pasta in the trash, we regroup. There's a smell of rain. The air is heavy, and the counsellors look up at the sky. A storm is close, but it might hold off until we're done, they say. The aim of the game is to get as close as possible to the lantern. If the guardian of the lantern hears you coming, he turns his torch on you and you have to go back to Base One. The first person to touch the lantern wins points for the team. Whoop-whoop!

"Stick together, teamsters," we're told. "And no talking or flashlights, else you'll give yourselves away." The counsellors fan out on the boundaries with torches. They'll make sure we don't wander off too far.

As soon as the counsellors have disappeared from Base One, my team splits up. Along with the other badasses, Dikeledi and Tebogo duck behind the kitchen block with a bottle of vodka. Xoliswa hurries back to the dormitory to take a shower – leaving me with Soo Ling.

"Hey, Jenna, where are you?"

"Shuddup, Soo, he'll hear us. Just stick with me, okay?" A few metres up the mountain, I slip behind a tree and ditch

Soo Ling. Bleat-bleat-bleat. I ignore her and run.

I race towards the light glowing in the distance. The sky is black, clouds have gathered, hiding the moon. The stars have fled.

I stumble past a giggling group of shadows. The butch girls are in a huddle, pretending they aren't making out. A little way on I smell cigarette smoke. Someone coughs. Not all the team builders are stalking the lantern. But I am.

I hurry towards the silhouette up ahead of me, swerve off to the left, and crouch down. Andile is standing at the mouth of the cave, looking out over my head. I scrabble on the ground, feel a stone under my fingers and toss it. It lands a couple of feet to my right and he turns, taking a few steps forward.

Now's my chance. I leap up and sprint towards the light. My fingers are within inches of the lantern – I so nearly touch the glass. But not.

"Ha, caught you! Back to Base One, Jen." Andile laughs as he shines a torch in my face. "But well done, you almost had me."

I fall to my knees and give a low groan.

"You all right?" He walks towards me. "You hurt yourself?"

Drops of rain wet my face as I look up to the light. "It's just … my ankle. Yes, my ankle. I think I've twisted it."

Andile's hand hesitates on my shoulder, then he lifts me up. Both hands are under my armpits, and the touch of his fingers send shivers down my neck. He drapes my arm around his shoulder and we hobble towards the entrance of the cave. The rain splatters my feet, lightning flashes in the sky. The thunder roars above our heads.

We are no sooner inside than there is the sound of whistles from below. Game over. The signal to regroup at Base One.

"I don't think I can walk right now." I wince.

"No problem, Jen. We'll wait for the storm to pass."

We sit in silence, listening to the rain coming down in front of the cave.

"You doing okay there, Jen? Not too much pain, I hope?"

"I'm freezing." I really am. Hands around my knees, I stare into the blackness and the wet.

"Here, take this." He hands me his sweatshirt. *No, I never went to Berkeley, OK.* It's one of my favourites. I smell him as I pull it over my T-shirt. He's not a cologne kind of a guy, it's apple shampoo and sweat.

"I need to tell Base One we're safe." Andile takes out his phone. No signal. I slide mine out and sneak a sideways pic of our faces.

Click.

The rain's still coming down. Please don't stop. Ever. I'm cold, I'm exhausted, and I'm damn uncomfortable. I'm with Andile, and I'm in heaven.

Next afternoon, the bus drops the Team Builders of the Future off at school. I hang around outside Reception with Soo Ling and some of the others until Holly eventually pitches up. She's wearing her Trust Me To Sell Your

Beautiful House outfit. Heels, tailored linen suit. And no bra.

I'm not the only one who notices Holly's perky chest – or her legs. She's not so popular with the other moms, though she's far too popular with their husbands. They all walk past us, their eyes moving from her neck to her knees and finally her face. They don't look her in the eye.

"Don't forget this, Jen," says Andile. "And make sure you see a doctor about that ankle." He hands me my sleeping bag and his eyes light on Holly. They don't stop at her face. He smiles at her. "Sorry, I'm grubby. Camp, you know. I'm Andile Skhosana, Jen's history teacher." He reaches out his hand, Holly's rests in it. "Eish, you and Jen are like two peas." His eyes flick from her to me and back again, lingering on Holly.

Soo Ling giggles next to me. "Which of the Moore girls does Randy Andy like best, I wonder?" Her eyes gleam with spite. "I'd say your mom's got him whipped."

Pushing past Holly as she tries to hug me, I forget to limp. I throw my stuff on the back seat of the car. I hate her, I hate her, I hate her.

I close the pizza box and prop my foot up on the couch as Holly chatters away on her phone. I hadn't figured on Barry being such a conversationalist, but for sure, he's a member of Toastmasters. She finally ends the call and comes through to the lounge. "Your teacher says hello. I told him I'd let him know what Doctor Levine says tomorrow. If you make the appointment, I'll take you."

What the heck?

"Andile phoned? Why didn't you call me?"

"Baby, he didn't ask for you. He just wanted to make sure with me that you're okay." I'm hating that smile on Holly's lips. She parks herself on a chair, taps away at her phone as she says, "He must have got my number from the school."

I limp off to my bedroom and check Facebook. Andile's got a new friend: Holly Moore. No, this can't be happening. She's posted on his wall: Ordinary people have big TVs. Extraordinary people have big libraries.

Seriously? Is Holly pretending to be a reader? When she's not out partying she's on the couch hogging the remote, watching endless reality shows about obese people and crazy hoarders. Or it's an inside joke. I don't get it.

Does Andile get it? Is he smiling as he reads this? Did he tell Holly he had a big library, or is Holly making one of those smutty jokes? The two of them have pushed me into the naughty corner and turned their backs on me as they giggle.

There's only one thing to do. I post two photos on Facebook. Andy and me at his flat after breakfast. I had seconds. Delicious! Also: Andy and me take shelter in a cave. So snug!

Holly will definitely see them. She must learn that when it comes to Andile, I'm first. She must get the hell away. I watch the screen. Within minutes I have twenty likes and four comments from my fellow Virgins:

Hot Stuff!

Baybeeeee! You got a cute boyf!

127

Way to go, girl!

Beauuuuutiful couple!

I take a bath, wallowing as I wash the camp dirt away. After towelling myself dry, I call Andile. I sometimes do this just to hear his voice. My number is set on private so he doesn't know. His phone goes straight to voicemail:

Hi there, I can't take your call, but leave a message and maybe I'll get back to you.

There's a beep and I end the call.

I check Facebook again. Two hundred and twenty likes, seventy-three comments, and eighteen shares. My chest explodes as I scroll down:

He's your teacher, that's not cool! Frowning emoticon.

What's the prison sentence for statutory rape? Angry emoticon.

Hey Jenna, you're only fifteen, right? Wow.

Who are all these people commenting on my life? I don't even know them. I delete the photos, but it's too late. They're out there. Shared with hundreds of strangers. I switch off my phone and bury my face in Andile's sweatshirt.

MARGARET

Mrs Schaumbacher is taking us to the Top Star Drive-In for a double feature tonight. Goody, goody gumdrops.

Gemima has packed the usual: a thermos of Koffiehuis, chicken pieces, and a bag of popcorn each for Benny and me. Mrs Schaumbacher doesn't touch the stuff. She says the pips get stuck in her bridge.

When I'm big I'm never going to pack food when I go to the drive-in. I'm always going to buy from their take-away café. The burgers squirt delicious fatty juice as you bite into them. My mother says drive-in food is common.

I haven't seen much of Benny lately. He's been doing lots of errands with his mother and hasn't been able to walk home with me after school. Some days I see their Peugeot parked in the driveway, but when I go next door Mavis says she doesn't know where they are or when they'll be back.

This one time I saw Mrs Schaumbacher getting dropped off a few houses down the road in a car like Roger the Dodger's but not as clapped-out. She wobbled up the road in high heels and was wearing a big coat. A scarf was wrapped across her face. She had sunglasses like Jackie Kennedy in America, even though it was getting dark.

I ran to meet her. "Hey, Mrs Schaumbacher, I hardly recognised you!"

She took off her sunglasses. Her eyes were pink. It could have been conjunctivitis or an allergy to washing powder, I wasn't sure. She gave a funny laugh and a sigh. "Well, good. That's the idea."

I didn't ask her what she meant. My father told me after I found Mr Schaumbacher in our garden that I shouldn't ask Benny and his mother too many questions. Times being a bit difficult, and so forth.

It's still light as we take the road to the drive-in on the top of the mine dump.

We're off to see the Wild West show-ho-ho. The elephant and the kangaroo-hoo-hoo-hoo. Never mind the weather, as long as we're together …

Benny and I sing along as Mrs Schaumbacher drives like a tortoise, and she keeps looking in the rear-view mirror. She's a considerate driver, not like Lucy, who is a demon. Benny and I kneel on the back seat. We look out the window and stick our tongues out at the passing cars.

The man at the entrance to the drive-in stretches his neck as he looks into our car. Mrs Schaumbacher passes some notes and a few coins through the hole in his cubicle. "One adult and two children." The man leans forward again, and I lift the blanket off our knees so he can see we haven't smuggled anyone in.

He waves us through. "Have a lekker evening."

We drive off in search of a spot. "Not too far from the toilets in case I need to go," I say to Mrs Schaumbacher. I always need to wee. The average amount of urine excreted in twenty-four hours is between five and eight cups. My bladder is the size of a peanut.

Mrs Schaumbacher finds a parking place. She rolls her window halfway down and clips the speaker onto it. She switches the sound on.

"It's too crackly, we need to find a better spot," I say.

She doesn't seem to hear me. She adjusts her seat so that it leans back. Benny and I are going to have to take turns sitting behind her because of her beehive hairstyle. She thinks she's made of glass.

The first film on the programme comes after a Laurel and Hardy cartoon. It's *The Comancheros*, with John Wayne and Stuart Whitman. I'm quite mad for John, who's a Texas ranger. Benny rates Stuart best. He's not that keen on policemen, and he reckons John's a spaz for not knowing Stuart was a good guy all along.

We finish the chicken – I get the wishbone, but I don't let Benny help pull it. We give Mrs Scahumbacher the Pope's nose because Benny and me know it's the chicken's bum and we won't touch it.

Halfway through the first show, Mrs Schaumbacher says she's going to powder her nose.

"I need to go too," I say.

"Well, let me go first, Margaret, and then you can go and I'll stay with Benny."

"Mummy says I mustn't ever go alone."

"Well, you can tell your mother from me that she's sewing straight. Benny will go with you, but in the meantime wait here with him."

Mrs Schaumbacher climbs out of the driver's seat, shuts the door and fiddles with the speaker on the window. It's still crackly, even when I jiggle it while she's busy in the boot. I watch her walk off with a small suitcase in her hand.

"What's your mom got in that case?" I say.

"Shoosh, man, I'm trying to watch."

Benny's eyes are glued to the screen. He's seen the film twice before at the Colosseum and knows it off by heart. His hand is shovelling in popcorn so fast it's going to be finished by the time the second feature starts. He'd better not beg for some of mine.

I finish off the coffee but I'm still thirsty. Gemima always puts too much salt in the popcorn. Mrs Schaumbacher has brought a bottle of Lecol orange juice. I drink more than my share, and cross my legs tightly. I really, really have to go.

"Benny, I have to wee. You must come with." I punch him on the arm a couple of times, giving him a lamey.

He pulls a face and puts on his slippers. Together we wander off towards the toilet block. The huge screen lights up the lawn in front of it. Bodies lie stretched out on blankets, or lean into each other. They don't seem to care about what John and Stuart are getting up to on the screen. When I'm as old as Lucy, I'm never going to sit in the car. I'll always sit on the grass in the open air. But there's no way I'm going to kiss some disgusting boy.

I wait in the queue outside the *Ladies/Dames* block as Benny slips inside an entrance that smells like Jeyes Fluid. On his way out, he grins at me. "I'll be waiting for you by the café. Maybe I'll get us some chips." He rattles the coins in his dressing-gown pocket. "Make sure you don't go back to the car without me. Mummy won't like it." The way he says "Mummy" I want to lamey his other arm too. But I don't want to lose my place in the queue.

When I walk back from the toilet, I look at the people lying on the grass again. I notice a lady and a man sitting with their knees up, talking to each other. They're not watching the film either. The man stands and picks up a suitcase. His bald head shines in the light from the screen. He bends down, touches the lady on her shoulder, and she holds on to his fingers. As he walks away, she gets up and brushes bits of grass from her skirt. It's Mrs Schaumbacher.

Benny's not at the café so I hurry back to the car. I'm already inside when Mrs Schaumbacher says, "Your turn, Margaret." I tell her my wee has gone away and it's okay. The car smells of chips and vinegar. Benny offers me some. He grips the bottom end of the bag so I can't take more than my share.

Mrs Schaumbacher is quiet the whole way through the next film. It's *One Hundred and One Dalmatians*. At the end, she bursts into tears.

We drive off and Benny reaches up and puts a hand on her cheek. She puts a hand over it, letting it slide down when she has to change gears. Then she takes Benny's hand in her own again. She cries the whole way home.

I don't know why. It's not like any of the dogs died.

On Sundays I always help Gemima make my father's breakfast. She lets me stir the oats and flip his eggs. She'll soon be off to church with Sophie and the methodical Methodists. Sometimes I help her with the dishes so she can finish at the double and go, but not if my mother is around. She's upstairs, though, dressing for church. Gemima got me ready ages ago. I'm glad Benny doesn't go to Mass with me. He'd tease me about the mantilla my mother makes me wear on my head.

My father puts the *Sunday Times* down on the table and says: "Ntombi?"

"More coffee, Doctor?"

He shakes his head and gives her a worried look. "You didn't go to the post office yesterday, did you?"

"You want me to post something for you? Our queue was so long I have to go back tomorrow for stamps."

"You mean you didn't post my letters this week? There were four of them." I frown at Gemima. "Why didn't you go earlier? Lazybones."

She frowns back at me. "They closed before I got to the front of my queue. Yours was short, you could have bought stamps quick-quick. The letters must wait until tomorrow."

My father gives the newspaper a tap and says, "Well, looks like they won't be selling stamps at our post office for a while. I'll have to post our letters in town."

I reach over and take a squizz at the front page. Then I see the headline, it's at the bottom, next to the advert showing a family bathing their dog: *United – largest South African building Society*. I read out loud: "Home-made bomb shatters postbox". A bit below the headline, it says: "*The bomb caused extensive damage to the post office soon after it was closed yesterday morning.*" And bags of letters were blown to pieces, all over the pavement.

"Why did someone bomb our postbox?" I ask my father.

"It's complicated, Mags." He takes the newspaper from me. "The person who planted the bomb was angry, but not with you. It exploded before he could get away, and so he lost his life."

Things like this often happen in cartoons at the bioscope, like when Wile E Coyote plays with explosives trying to catch the Road Runner. He ends up blowing himself up and then he's all fine and ready to go again in the next one.

Gemima makes a funny noise. Her head is bent over the sink. She looks like she's praying.

I get up from the table and put my arms around her. She's all shivery. "Don't worry, Mima, the bomb didn't get my letters. Daddy can post them for me tomorrow."

JENNA

I run from the house, leaving a note for Holly on the fridge. *Got an early appointment with Doctor Levine. See you after school.*

The security guy at the end of the street is leaning back in his chair, eyes closed, his face raised to the early morning sun. The dew makes the electric fences spark along the tops of the walls. Tick-tick-tick.

Where can I go? Not school. No, not there. I don't have money for a taxi, though in any case I can't face hiding out in a mall. But there's one place no one will find me.

I wave at Obvious and let myself into 37 Klip Street. My breathing slows as I punch in the security code. Home safe.

I stand in the main bedroom. A quilt is folded at the end of the double bed. It's hand-stitched, and attached to it is a piece of fabric with *For Dianne 2008* handwritten in black. A labour of love.

Mr Fram's a good husband. Mrs Fram calls him Bobby or Bob, and sometimes Robert. *Darling Bobby, I left your supper in the oven. See you later. D. xxx.* Another note on the fridge reads: *Robert, please deal with the insurance company. They have called four times.*

I wander into James's bedroom. The book I'd left for him on my last visit is still on the bookshelf. I know he'll love it when he reads it one day. I know everything about James. He doesn't eat raisins. His favourite food is spaghetti. I bet he likes the sound it makes when he sucks it into his mouth. His Grade Three teacher's name is Miss Davis and he loves her. He's drawn a picture of Miss Davis and attached it to the fridge with a magnet. He's given her yellow hair and a crown. He doesn't colour inside the lines.

I lie on James's bedroom floor, hugging his crocodile, waves of panic washing over me whenever I think about my Facebook page. Everyone at school will have seen the photos. It's all over Instagram, Snapchat, WhatsApp, Twitter. Of course, people took screenshots and shared my post before I deleted it – it's everywhere, I can never erase it. I've really blown it. Perhaps if I don't say anything it will all go away. Facebookers have short attention spans.

My phone rings. I reach for it in my satchel but it's crammed with stuff. Maybe Andile is trying to get hold of me? I dump the contents on the carpet and scrabble about. It's just Holly. I mute the ringtone. As I shove the stuff back inside I spot the autograph book I'd nicked from Pembroke Street. I never did get a chance to ask Andile to sign it.

Inside the cover it says: *Lucy Channing-Court.* This is crossed out, and underneath is written: *This book NOW belongs to Margaret Beatrice Channing-Court.*

I flip through the pastel pages: Someone's drawn a heart

with an arrow pointing downwards, signed: *Your classmate Louise Daincroft*. Further on, I read:

> *Dear Mad Mags,*
> *Wen you get old and think your sweet,*
> *just take off your shoos and smel yor feet.*
> *From Benjamin Schaumbacher, 26 Pembroke Street (nex dor to you)*

At the sound of voices I leap up and look out the window. Mr and Mrs Fram are walking up the path towards the front door. I stuff the book into my satchel, run to the kitchen and slip out of the back. I make sure the door locks behind me.

The Frams will notice that the alarm system's been deactivated. They might even call Holly to complain. Obvious is sure to tell them I've been there. Give up, Jenna, you're screwed. Can I possibly be in any worse trouble than I'm already in?

MARGARET

Gemima lays three coins at the end of my bed every Monday morning. One for the poor, one for the pig, and one for me.

My father gives me pocket money every week and I can spend it any way I choose, except on comics. I sometimes read Benny's at his house but I don't dare bring them home. *Look and Learn* is the only magazine my mother allows me to buy.

No *Beano* or *Archie* for me. I must only read proper books from the library or wait for my parcel of Enid Blytons and Nancy Drews from my grandmother in England. A few weeks ago my mother insisted I read *Little Lord Fauntleroy*. It was ghastly. Cedric calls his mother "Dearest" and he even wears ringlets. He's a real drip.

It's jolly annoying that Gemima doesn't have a library card. I can only take out two books a week, and I'm not allowed to borrow from the adult section. Gemima never reads anything except the Bible. Also, apart from using the Ann Wise column, all she does with newspapers is cut them into squares for her lavatory.

I slip one of the coins into my piggy bank. When it's full, my father will take me to the United Building Society and they'll cut open its stomach and put the money into my account.

Sometimes I get desperate towards the end of the week and I stick a butter knife into the slot in the pig's head, and a coin slides out. Benny says if I carry on stealing from the pig I'm never going to get rich. My mother says Benny talks like a real whatchamacallit.

It's tuckshop at school today. Sister Athanasius is Tickey Sister and sells loose Wilson's toffees and liquorice. Sister Francesca is Sixpence Sister, with hot dogs, chocolate bars and flavoured milk. No fizzy drinks or eskimo pies. We have to buy these from Louis the Greek at the corner café. It's got a pinball machine, but the boys never give me a chance to play.

At the entrance to the church is the Poor Box. Every week I put a coin into it. Not today, though. Benny's mother isn't giving him pocket money any more as things are a bit tight since Mr Schaumbacher left home and isn't around to bring home the bacon. I'm going to lend Benny my Poor Box coin and I'm not going to charge him interest. He can do my arithmetic homework instead.

At break, I can't find Benny. I wander around like a spare wheel. The girls in the playground are playing elastics, their school dresses tucked into their bloomers. *Jingle jangle, centre spangle. Jingle Jangle Out.* I sing along under my breath. *England, Ireland, Scotland, Wales. Inside, outside, puppy dogs' tails.*

Another group are skipping with a long rope. *All in together, dusty, dusty weather. I spy Jack, peeping through the crack.* There's a girl holding each end, and together they turn the rope. The rest line up and take turns to jump. Faster and faster it turns, and the girl has to skip faster and faster – until she trips and is out. I'm dying to play, but they won't ever ask me.

At last I find Benny by the tennis court, surrounded by a group of boys. They're all Standard Fives. One of the bigger boys sticks his chin out so that it almost touches Benny's face. "Hey, you want to see Durban? Hey, do you, Hairy-lip?"

Benny tries to smile. I can see he's not sure if he wants to see Durban. I've been there lots of times when we go to my Uncle Frank's farm, but Benny hasn't. His family usually goes to Plettenberg Bay in the Cape. Last Christmas Benny didn't go anywhere because his father had to stay in Johannesburg and there was no getting round it. My father said the reason for it was difficult to explain, and so forth.

"So. Do you? Want to see Durban, hey?" It doesn't sound like the boys are giving Benny any choice, and one of them moves in close.

"No, he doesn't. Go away." I push them aside and stand next to Benny. I know what the bully wants to do. He's going to hold Benny's head with both hands and lift him up into the air and say: "Look, there's Durban." It's really not funny and it hurts your neck like blazes.

"Maybe Fang here wants to see Canada instead? Like his father." One of the boys waves a rolled-up newspaper in Benny's face. He jumps around, pretending it's a sword.

"My dad says your dad is a dirty commie and deserves to hang with the rest of the kaffirs." He smacks Benny on the top of his head with the newspaper while the other boys laugh.

I snatch the newspaper out of the boy's hand. "Mr Schaumbacher is an architect, not a commie. He doesn't even speak Russian. So there." I toss the newspaper on the ground and drag Benny off to get some sherbet from Tickey Sister. When I suck the sherbet through the straw and blow out, it looks like I'm smoking, like Lucy.

Our last class for the day is English spelling. Sister Columbanus opens the dictionary and chooses a word. She picks on someone and if you get it wrong, you have to try another word. Three wrong answers in a row earns you the ruler.

"Outrageous." And then she looks around the classroom, her hand holding the silver cross at her neck. Her face is red. "Benny Schaumbacher." She always picks on him, never any of the other boys.

Benny stands and tries to spell the word. Out-rage-ous. It's eezy peezy puddysticks, but I never get chosen. He gets the first bit right, but loses his way after "rage".

"Come up here." Sister Columbanus puts the dictionary on her table and picks up a newspaper. She skims the front page, her eyes like angry black flies. She tosses it away, rubs her fingers together.

"Communist." Sister Columbanus waits as Benny walks to the front of the classroom. He looks out over our heads. I try to catch his attention. My fingers sign the deaf alphabet.

I learnt it at Brownies and taught him so he knows it like the back of his hand.

"Imposter." Sister Columbanus shakes Benny by the shoulders. "I said: 'Imposter'." She picks up the newspaper again, points to the headline and shouts: "Communist slips police net." She throws the newspaper aside and grabs the ruler. It comes down hard on Benny's legs. Again and again. The metal end makes stripes on his skin.

"Now go back to your desk!"

Benny doesn't move. He turns to Sister Columbanus and says, "But you never finished the sentence: 'Communist slips police net and escapes to Bechuanaland' – to freedom, Sister. F. R. E. E. D. I. M."

Ag no, Benny! He's spelt it wrong. Why does he always falter at the last hurdle?

Sister Columbanus reaches for the ruler again and shrieks: "D.O.M. Free-dom-dom-dom." She says it like the Afrikaans word for "dumb". The ruler slams down three more times on Benny's legs. "You dimwit." Her face is full of splotches. They look like cumulus clouds just before a thunderstorm.

Benny limps back to his desk, his lip lifted in a smile.

After doing my homework, I go over to Benny's and find him and his mother in the front room. The radio is on, and Mrs Schaumbacher is dabbing Mercurochrome on Benny's cuts. She mutters "Columbanus" with each dab. The way Benny says her name: "Columb-Anus". The jingle plays, it's the six o'clock news. Short pips – peep, peep, peep – and one long one: peeeeep.

"Move over, Scumbucket, you're taking up all the space."
I push him, trying to make myself comfortable on the couch.

"Shoosh, Margaret, we want to hear the news." Mrs
Schaumbacher is wringing her hands like they're a wet lappie.

Benny and Mrs Schaumbacher hardly breathe until the
newsreader has finished. Mrs Schaumbacher throws her arms
around Benny. "It's true. Your dad's safely in Canada ."

Benny bursts into tears. I turn away so he doesn't get
embarrassed. I also cry when bad things happen and I hate it
when people stare at me. "But I thought it was good news?"

Mrs Schaumbacher switches off the wireless, cutting the
weather report. Now I won't know if there is a likelihood of
rain in Griqualand West. Or if there's a gale warning. "Yes,
Margaret. It is good news. It's the very best." She's crying too,
but she's also smiling. She hands Benny a handkerchief.
"Buck up, darling. It's nearly over."

The phone rings and Mrs Schaumbacher jumps up. Their
phone is working perfectly for a change, because she has a
jolly long conversation. "Eh, Benny," she calls out, "someone
wants to say 'How ya doin?'." She's giggling like Louise
Daincroft when I shove my ruler under her bottom.

I can't hear what Benny says on the phone, but when he
comes back he says he's ready to beat me at Monopoly. I crow
like a witch when he lands on Mayfair Street and he has to
cough up for my hotel. But Benny doesn't sulk and doesn't
seem to care when I take all his money and say, "I'm the
winner!"

Before I go to bed, I cut a photograph of Mr

Schaumbacher out of the *Rand Daily Mail.* My father said I could because he'd finished reading it. I slip the photo into the pages of my Dorland's medical dictionary. I'll keep it to remind Benny of the day he got more stripes on his legs than anyone in the history of our school. It's an enviable achievement.

Underneath the photo it says: *Disguised like this, Mr Leonard Schaumbacher crossed the border.* I hardly recognise him. He's doesn't have a beard, and he's wearing a veil, like a nun. His habit is hitched up to his knees, showing his hairy legs. He's smiling and smoking a cigarette and holding up a glass.

He's the prettiest penguin I've ever seen.

JENNA

Where to go? Where to go?

There's Pembroke Street, of course. No one will come looking for me there. I cross the road at an intersection, dodging cars. The traffic snarls and hoots all the way down Sylvia Pass. I reach the house and give a limp wave to Clever, who salutes me with a smile. I call Aunt C-C, and after a few long minutes she answers and says, "Jenny? I wasn't expecting you until this afternoon." This time, I don't bother to correct her.

"There's no school today." I hesitate, searching for the right words. "It's some kind of public holiday, I think." Holly's lying gene has gone rampant, I realise.

There is a silence at the end of the phone. "I'm not sure if that is correct. Sharpeville Day is the week after next. Well, Human Rights Day as it is now called." A pause, then, "Fine, I'll open up."

She's dressed for an outing. Her hair is puffed up in fluffy curls, and her cheeks are heavily powdered. A cameo brooch is pinned to her collar, which sags at her scrawny neck.

"Hey, you're looking all gussied up. Going on a date?" I'm out of breath, my eyes smarting from the car exhaust fumes.

My head is floating off my neck.

She gives me an annoyed look. "Well, I do have an appointment. But now that you're here, you may as well come inside."

I follow her through to the kitchen and she switches on the kettle. She sets the tray with the teapot, the beaded doily, the white cups and saucers. I watch her as she busies herself and my heartbeat slows.

"One for you, one for me, and one for the pot." She puts three spoonfuls of tea into the warmed pot. "How was camp? You got back yesterday?"

"You know, camp," I shrug.

"They made us do all kinds of ghastly physical exercise in my day, I recall. Obstacle courses and environmental treasure hunts and day-long hikes. Activities designed to make us compete, setting us at each other's throats." She gives the pot a quick stir. "Those ridiculous gold stars. I don't think I ever got one. And the never-ending prayers before lights-out."

"Yip, that's camp."

Waving my hand away, she takes the tray through to a room off the passage. "This was my father's study. I always feel a little like I'm intruding when I'm in here. Silly, really, I know he wouldn't mind."

A filing cabinet stands against the wall, magazines and books fill the shelves. A mahogany desk dominates the room. On it, a framed photograph of two unsmiling children: a chubby-kneed boy in a sailor suit, and next to him a skinny black girl wearing long white socks and lace-up shoes. In a sack-like dress that seems to hang on her, she stands with one hand on his shoulder.

A state-of-the-art iMac blinks at me from the centre of the desk.

"Could I ask you to play mother – I need to send off a rather urgent email." Aunt C-C looks up and sees the disbelief on my face. "What I mean is, would you mind pouring the tea."

"Wow! You've got a computer."

"It's the way to go if one wishes to stay in touch with the world." Her tone is dry, it's as if she's laughing at me. She sits down, her fingers resting on the keyboard. "I can't tolerate all this social media nonsense. I did try Myspace a few years ago and was besieged with friend requests from people I regret ever knowing. But the google and email are marvellous. I don't know why we bother with the post office any more."

"It's Facebook now," I blurt. My stomach clenches. Stop. Box that thought. "Ja, Facebook and Snapchat and Instagram and Twitter and Tumblr." I'm babbling. "Oh, and Holly swears by Tinder." I pour the tea, add a dash of milk, and wait for a snide comment about Holly and dating.

"I know all about the Facebook and so on. I do live in the twenty-first century, you know." Aunt C-C shuts down the computer and turns around. As I pick up my teaspoon and reach for the sugar bowl, she leans forward, her hand hovering over the bowl with its silver-crested spoon. "Here, let me help you. Will one do?"

I nod, and she watches as I give the tea a stir, the silver-crested spoon back where it belongs. I raise my cup. Cheers, Aunt C-C. Then I say, "You must have driven Holly nuts when she lived with you."

"It was a very long four years. I fear I lack the maternal instinct and was too hard on her." She takes a sip of her tea. "My own mother was a cold fish. This house was never warm. Holly might have been better placed with my sister in England. But my Uncle Frank wanted his only grandchild in South Africa. I agreed to take Holly on because he was simply too old to have her, and his wife – though comparatively young – was in poor health." She glances at her wrist. "My appointment is in half an hour, I don't want to be late."

"I expect she gave you a tough time too. Holly tells me she used to be really wild."

I don't add that Holly hasn't bucked the habit, but please, Aunt C-C, take the bait. Tell me about Holly's past – let's not talk the present, I live with it every day. Come on, tell me.

Aunt C-C dabs her lips with a handkerchief. "Oh, yes. She was ever so popular with the boys. Always out and about, I couldn't keep her home, much as I tried."

"Well, Holly's very easygoing with me. She lets me do pretty much anything I want."

"Now *that* is an interesting approach to parenting." She puts her cup down. "Are you also one for going to parties, and so forth, with boys?"

I shrug. It's not cool to admit that I never get asked out, and apart from Xoliswa's brothers, I don't know any boys.

There's just Andile. No, get a grip. Don't go there.

"I hang out with friends, and stuff. But at Virgins you don't get to meet many boys. Being an-all girls' school and all, you know."

"Virgins? What a thing to call my alma mater!" With a shake of her head she banishes the word. "Yet there was a time when St Virgilius did admit boys. They were schooled there for about a year following some catastrophic fire at the boys' college down the road. The penguins found it all rather trying."

"Penguins?"

I grin, and her cheeks flush. "It is what we girls called the nuns, Jenny. I don't think we meant any disrespect." She gets a faraway look, and says, "A friend who teaches at the school tells me that the nuns are long gone, and these days the church is only used for Sunday mass." After a pause, she turns to me again. "Your mother certainly didn't find this much of an obstacle. She always managed to find boys."

"Yes. She told me about Danny, who was at university with her. She told me all about him."

"Now there's a boy who squandered his youth." She clears her throat, looks at her watch again. "While I'm away, I want you to box the books and magazines in the study. When this is done, finish off with packing up the crockery in the lounge."

She stands up and pats her hair. "At any rate, I'm off. Don't forget to mark the boxes. I will be back shortly." She's out the front door before I can ask her where she's going and how she's getting there. She's too frail to drive a car, and God forbid she takes a minibus taxi!

As the door slams, my fingers fly to the filing cabinet. The top drawer is dusty, the files arranged alphabetically. I flick through: Bradley. Guthrie ... They're all empty.

The next drawer has less dust and files filled with bank statements and house insurance correspondence. One file is labelled *Discovery Health*, and it's stuffed with medical claims. Next to it, a file called *Hellkom* is full of Telkom correspondence – telephone and internet stuff. It's clear that Aunt C-C refuses to pay for shabby service.

A letter from the police. Ha, a jailbird in the family! I see it's addressed to Lucy Channing-Court. Dated 2 August 1963, it gives permission for "daily visits for the purpose of delivering food to the detainee and picking up laundry". But the prisoner's name is Roger Smythers. No relation, what a pity.

I slide the letter back and flip through the rest, my eye caught by a file marked *Jennifer Moore*. I check inside, my stomach knotting. Ag, no. My Virgins school reports. Right from Grade One. *Jenna must try harder; Jenna seldom hands in her projects; Jenna is an intelligent girl and could do so much better if she applied herself to her studies; Jenna does not pay attention in class.* Just another example of squandered youth. But why would Aunt C-C have these? And there's more: school fee statements show that Aunt C-C's been footing the bill. I was right, there's no way Holly could ever afford Virgins. Another of Holly's lies by omission. If this is Aunt

C-C's way of saying sorry to Holly for being such a cold fish, she shouldn't have bothered. Holly wanted nothing to do with her.

I look around the rest of the room, rummage through the desk drawers. No joy, though. I swallow down my cold tea and get on with packing the books. The journals date back seventy years or so, way before the link between smoking and cancer was discovered.

Like, duh!

I pack the journals and magazines into one box and the medical books into another. Most of this is of no use to anyone and belongs at the recycling dump. I pull out a pile of magazines and a book falls from the shelf, nearly braining me. As I pick the brute up, I notice the title: *Dorland's Illustrated Medical Dictionary*. Curious about the illustrations, I turn the page and notice the inscription:

> *Dearest Margaret,*
> *I wish you all the happiness on your eighth birthday.*
> *Love,*
> *Daddy*
> *24 February, 1962*

Whoa! Who'd give a book like this to an eight-year-old? Like, really? On her birthday? A newspaper cutting flutters from the pages. It's a photo of a man dressed like a nun. Naughty boy! I slip it inside again and drop the book into the box, which I mark with my pen.

I clear the tea things and take the tray to the kitchen. On my way back, the front door opens. I nearly have a heart attack. "Oh no, Miss Leventhorpe. What are *you* doing here?"

Behind her, Aunt C-C stumbles in through the front door. The brooch at her neck is hanging skew and her face is scary pale.

"I believe I could ask you the same question." Miss Leventhorpe hands Aunt C-C her bag and kisses her cheek. "Alrightie, darling, just take it easy. Those meds will knock the stuffing right out of you."

She takes me aside as Aunt C-C climbs the stairs without so much as a hello.

"I need to get back to school, I have a Grade Ten English class later this morning, as you well know. But your aunt needs a little looking after, the chemo really takes it out of her."

Chemo. The word is a kick in my gut. "Aunt C-C's got cancer?" I'd assumed she was moving to some kind of retirement home, but it seems she wasn't going anywhere after all.

"Ah well, she doesn't like to talk about it. Let her rest for a while, but keep an eye on her."

She shuts the door behind her and drives off. I go upstairs and peer into Aunt C-C's room. It's empty, the bedspread folded neatly on a nearby chair. In the bathroom I find her standing in front of the mirror, a razor lifted to her soapy head. Tears trickle down her cheeks, mucking up her powder.

"Jeez, what the heck do you think you're doing?"

"It's time I lost it all." She draws the razor across the top of her head. Tufts of hair fall into the basin.

"Listen, if you're going for a new look, at least let me help." I put the toilet seat down and give it a pat. "Come on, I've shaved Holly's legs loads of times. I'll be real careful." I tuck a towel around her neck. With her head poking through, she looks like a pigeon that's been buffeted by the wind.

Aunt C-C weeps as I shave. "My hair, my beautiful hair," she whispers.

I touch her shoulder. Please stop crying. Please. I dry her head. It's knobbly and veiny.

"You'll find a scarf in the bottom drawer of my dressing table," she says, her voice shaky.

I fetch the scarf and tie it onto her shiny dome. "It's very fashionable these days to wear a doek. I think I can make it work for you."

"A doek! My old nanny would have laughed. She always wore one."

"I don't think you look like a gogo. More like Audrey Hepburn. The one my grandfather was mad for." I grin at her. "Seriously, you look dope."

She arches an eyebrow. "You can stop this now, Jenny. I don't need all that nonsense. But … thank you." She stands in front of the mirror, puckers her lips and adjusts the scarf so that it looks like a turban. "Yes, as you say, quite … dope."

I help her into her bedroom and she lets me unpin the brooch. I unbutton the collar and she lies down. Taking the bedspread from the chair, I put it over her legs and begin to tuck it in.

"No, no, no. We can't have that. If you could just fold it up and put it back. I feel perfectly warm without it." Staring up at the ceiling, she says, "I think you can leave me now. I may just be able to sleep."

"I told Miss Leventhorpe I'd watch over you. I think I might hang around a bit."

"That will not be necessary. Mary Leventhorpe is a dear friend, but she tends to fuss. I'll be perfectly fine on my own. And in any case, you ought to be at school." She closes her eyes. "I wonder if you might ask your mother to pop around one day. When she's not too busy. She and I need to have a little chat."

"About her squandered youth? Hers and Danny's?"

Aunt C-C's eyes flutter open. "I did try to put a stop to it, you know. That boy was rotten and bent on self-destruction. Jenny, I believe that if it hadn't been for you, your mother would be dead too." She closes her eyes and sighs. "Yes, dead."

I walk home in a daze. Holly is pacing the kitchen, picking at her turquoise fingernails.

"Where the hell have you been? I've been going out of my mind."

I push past her. "Get off my case."

"Excuse me! Excuse me, missy!" She shouts after me, "Hey, you, get right back here. Your mother wants a word with you."

"My mother?" I stop and face her. "Sorry, Holly, it's a bit late to lay that mumsy crap on me."

"Jenna, please. We need to talk."

I give her a glare, then hurry away and lock my door. I put in my earphones and turn up the volume. I pull the pillow over my head, ignoring the thumps on my door. I'd waited and hoped for so long, and it's all been pointless. My father's dead, and I never even got to meet him. And he never got to decide if he even wanted me.

MARGARET

I watch Charles taking a sand bath in Mrs Schaumbacher's agapanthus bed then stare at the sky, begging it to rain. It's as blue as the blue of Our Lady's shawl in the picture in Mother Superior's office. No sign of clouds.

The Yeoville pool opened two weeks ago on the first of September as usual. Benny has a pool and I'm dying to swim, but my mother says I'm not allowed before the first summer rains. That's the official start of the swimming season, according to my mother.

I collect pompoms under the itchy-ball tree and break them open into my handkerchief. I'll go find Benny, and when he's not looking I'll shove some of the fluff down the back of his shirt. He'll scratch himself to death.

I throw myself against the Schaumbachers' front door. Maybe it'll skrik Benny, he's such a scaredy-cat. I try the door, but it's locked. Behind it, the radio is blaring. Eventually, Mrs Schaumbacher lets me in. "Ag, shame. Sorry, Margaret. Benny's got a thing about locking the doors these days."

Lucy's in the front room.

"What you doing here, Luce?"

Lucy turns down the radio, and the voice stops singing

"Are You Lonesome Tonight?" She doesn't answer me and puts her coffee cup down on a table covered in greyish ring marks. Mrs Schaumbacher doesn't bother with coasters.

I spot a letter from Lucy's Canadian pen pal among some sewing patterns. The stamps show geese flying across the sky. I don't mind Lucy stealing my idea because she always gives me the stamps. She tells me her pen pal's name is Monica. But I never see her writing back, even though the letters come like clockwork, every single day.

"Hey," I say, reaching for the envelope, which is nice and fat. "I've got first dibs on those stamps. You're not giving them to Benny, are you?"

Lucy just sits there, without saying a word.

"Leave it right there, Margaret," says Mrs Schaumbacher as she slides the envelope away. "I'll make sure you get the stamps. Now run along. Benny's outside by the pool. I said he could put his feet in. Just his feet, mind you. Not a stitch more." Mrs Schaumbacher has the same swimming rule as my mother.

As I skip down the passage to the kitchen door, I spot a dangling cord. The telephone's been unplugged, and Benny's blazer's lying on top of it. The phone must be giving them problems again.

Benny's lying like a fat lizard on the slasto, catching a farmer tan. He's even wearing his socks and shoes. If I get him to play catches around the pool, maybe I'll accidentally fall in.

In the middle of the night, a family of giants begins to bounce all over our roof like it's a trampoline. But I open my eyes and realise that it's really just water pouring down from the clouds. Lightning cracks, thunder rolls over terrified skies, and hailstones the size of the diamond in the Queen's crown crash down. I crouch at my window watching the storm, my body trembling, too excited to go to sleep again.

In the morning, my mother's cannas lie bleeding and daffodils are scattered and squashed. After school, I go over to Benny's and manage to jump in the pool before he does. I swim three lengths underwater, without coming up for air once.

The next few weeks, Benny and I spend every day after school in the pool. My hair turns green and my skin gets wrinkly like Zacharias's bean seeds that he soaks before planting.

We can hear the shouting behind our back fence. Gavin Rademeyer also has a swimming pool, and they're all Marco Polo-ing and dive-bombing from the tree house. The mothers don't let them swim at Benny's because the Schaumbachers allow the children of their African friends to swim in their pool. I've swum with them lots of times, and I didn't even get a tiny bit sick.

There's no school today. Mother Superior sent our parents a letter saying it's best we stay at home. It's not because the Sub A pupils have lice again, it's in case of trouble. God willing, the police will keep the natives in order and things will be back to normal soon, my mother said.

I say a few prayers for trouble because a few days off school will save my life. I'm far behind on my sewing project. Last week Sister Mary Liguori unpicked my stitches and said, "That girl of yours won't be wearing her apron this century unless you master the daisy stitch. Now put your head down, and get this finished!"

If I have to go to school tomorrow and hand in my apron I'll get a hundred lines. I hope God understands my point of view and lets the trouble last. Miss van Tonder told us it's all about some cheeky Bantu who'll be in court today and everyone is worried the natives are going to riot and chase us out of our houses and burn down the country.

I won't be at home, in any case. Mrs Schaumbacher is taking Benny and me to the Snake Park outside Johannesburg. She has an errand to run in Pretoria and she's going to drop us off on the way there. Gemima's coming along to take care of us because their Mavis has taken off a few days and gone to her kraal for a funeral.

I went to the Snake Park a few years ago with my father and we watched the snake show. An African stood in the snake pit, holding a cobra. He pinched the back of its head until it showed its poisonous fangs. The cobra bit into the top of a covered cup. The fangs pierced the plastic and the venom dripped into the cup. It was brilliant. The African told us the Cape cobra's bite was deadly, but the Snake Park had anti-venom in the freezer for in case. My father told me it would be tickets for the African if that snake bit him because it was actually the *naja philippinensis* from the Philippines and they don't stock the antidote in South Africa. When I told Benny about it his face went green with envy.

We leave for the Snake Park after Gemima has hung out the washing. The Peugeot drives down Louis Botha Avenue, stopping every now and then at the traffic lights. Africans are just wiping shop windows and sweeping pavements, and no one is rioting.

We are marching to Pretoria, Pretoria, Pretoria. We are marching to Pretoria, Pretoria todaaay. Benny and I sing as we pass businesses selling things for the garden, painted gnomes and fences made of concrete wagon-wheels. We're almost at the Doll House. A sign says: *No Hooting. Please Flick Lights.* If you hoot, they won't come and clip a food tray to your window. I hammer against the driver's seat. "Milkshake time!" Benny joins me and we chant: "Milkshake, milkshake, milkshake!"

"Perhaps on the way back, if you've been very good." The car speeds up.

Gemima is in the front of the car. She usually sits in the back when my father gives her a lift, but I don't mind. We're playing cat's cradle, so our arms are out, making different shapes with our string. Gemima needs extra room – she's embroidering my apron for tomorrow's lesson. Just in case God and the natives let me down.

I make Diamonds. Benny's turn. Candle. I do Cradle. We keep going – and then Benny makes Two Crowns. I punch my fist through the string and shout, "You lose!"

Mrs Schaumbacher slows down as we pass Alexandra location. There are hardly any trees, and smoke from the small houses smears the sky. She speeds up past the Johannesburg Drive-in, its huge screen looking down at us.

Benny's brought along a bag of Chappies. As a rule, he's forbidden to chew bubblegum because Mrs Schaumbacher says it'll make acid in his tummy and ruin his digestive tract. He's allowed today because of his father being in Canada. But I'm in charge.

I give him a Chappies and he unwraps it. His mouth turns down. Banana flavour, the worst. "Yellow, yellow, lucky fellow," I say with my sing-song voice. I know it annoys him. He chews hard then blows a big bubble. I swat it, and it gets caught up in my fingers so I have to give him another Chappies. Green. It's as bad as yellow, but that's the luck of the draw.

We drive past horses, and farm stalls selling eggs and honey. We pull up at the Snake Park, but there's a sign: *Closed for Maintenance.* The sign near the bench says: *Europeans Only/Slegs Blankes.* Gemima would have been able to laze about on the grass and get on with my embroidery while Benny and I went to the snake show.

Mrs Schaumbacher puts her head on the steering wheel. Then she looks at her watch and says, "There's no time to take you children home again. You'll all have to come along."

She asks Gemima to sit in the back of the car with me. Gemima is hopeless at cat's cradle, but when I complain Mrs Schaumbacher holds up her hand like a traffic officer. "That's enough, Margaret. I have come to the end of my thread."

We cross a river, and Mrs Schaumbacher tells us it's the

Jukskei. We drive along a road with bluegum trees on either side. I see a sign saying *Halfway House* and I shout it out. "Yes, Margaret, we're halfway there. Now, please stop kicking my seat," she says. I see some mountains far away; they're the Magaliesberg, she tells us.

Further on, there's a big square building on a koppie, so I know we're almost in Pretoria. Most of the Afrikaans schools go there for outings, but my school always takes us to the War Museum in Saxonwold. It's not fair, but my mother says the Voortrekker Monument is for the Afrikaners, not for us. Afrikaner, vrot banana.

Mrs Schaumbacher drives past the big jail. Her shoulders are hunched as she grips the wheel.

I straighten the Chappies wrappers and make them into a small pile. Benny always gives his to me to read because of his spelling difficulties.

"Hey, Benny: 'Did you know? Athazagoraphobia is the fear of being forgotten or ignored?'" Benny doesn't say a word. "'Athazagoraphobia.' Did you hear me? I'm not asking you to spell it."

It's gone very quiet all of a sudden. I poke my head out of the window as the car slows down. Police cars and a big van are blocking the road. Policemen are stopping cars, and lots of buses filled with Africans are parked on the side.

Mrs Schaumbacher drives like a snail past some police vans, and then the car stops. A policeman's face is at my window, his eyes on Gemima in the back. He waves us to a spot next to the buses.

Mrs Schaumbacher stops on the gravel and winds down her window. "Yes, officer, can I help you?"

"Where you going?" The policeman stares hard at Gemima as she carries on with her daisy chain. Another one goes around to the back of the car and opens the boot.

Mrs Schaumbacher tells him we're on our way to the botanical gardens for a picnic. "Their school is closed today, so we're having an outing."

"And the kaffir girl. Where's she going?"

Mrs Schaumbacher says she's dropping Gemima off at the hospital to visit a sick aunt. The policeman says something in Afrikaans to his friend.

"What's wrong with her?" I say. It's the first I've heard of this.

Gemma slides her hand onto my knee and gives it a squeeze.

"Fine, I'll guess then. Something to do with the liver?"

She squeezes harder as she looks at the two policemen outside.

"Lungs?"

"Thula," she says. So I shut up.

The policeman turns to Mrs Schaumbacher and asks for identification. Gemima digs through her apron pocket and passes her little book across to Mrs Schaumbacher. The policeman's fingers flip through the pages, then he hands it back. "You need to avoid the centre of town," he says to Mrs Schaumbacher. "It's not safe today." He walks over to the car behind us as we pull away.

I grab the book as Mrs Schaumbacher passes it back, and page through. But who is Ntombifuthi Ndlovu? I point to the name and say, "Have you got someone else's book?"

Gemima snatches it from me. "That's me, it's my name." She blows her nose and looks away, then she turns to me. "Ntombifuthi means 'a girl again'. I was the sixth girl to be born, and my mother was out of patience. She wanted a son, you see." She puts the book in her pocket. "You've heard your daddy call me Ntombi. That's what my family calls me on the farm. Gemima is the name your mummy gave me when I came to work for her. She said it was easier."

My mother chose a jolly nice name. I wouldn't have wanted Gemima to be a Mavis or Sophie, which are very ordinary. I thank my lucky stars for my mother. It would have taken for ever and ever to embroider that other name on my apron.

I know what her surname means, and I begin to sing: "N-dlo-vu! E-le-phant! N-dlo-vu! E-le-phant! You're a big fat e-le-phant, Mima!" Gemima isn't laughing when she looks at me. So, very softly, I say, "Ndlovu. I love you. Ndlovu, I love you," until she smiles again.

Further on, we see more parked buses. Lots of Africans are standing about, some in groups. Policemen are looking through their little books – they're exactly like Gemima's! There's lots of shouting, and some Africans climb into the back of the police vans. The police wave their short black sticks around. We slow down, but this time no one stops us, and Mrs Schaumbacher drives on.

"Did you know? Bananas are slightly radioactive because they are rich in potassium?" I smooth my wrapper and pass Benny another Chappies. It's a pink one. "Pink, pink, you made a stink."

"I did not. A fox smells her own hole." He shoves it in his mouth before I can grab it back.

A little way on, closer to the centre of town, Mrs Schaumbacher parks the car. She sits a while, leaning back in her seat.

"Why are we waiting here?" I say. "I thought we were taking Mima to the hospital and going for a picnic?"

"I'm afraid there's no picnic today. I'm supposed to be meeting someone here, to drop off some food." She looks around, and has a worried look on her face. "He seems to be late, so we'll have to wait."

We stare at the people walking past, and then I say to Benny, "Let's play I Spy." I let him go first.

"I spy with my little eye, something beginning with G."

"Glove. Glovebox. Gum." Benny shakes his head. "Glass. Gum tree. Gutter." Four policemen jog past with dogs. "Gun, gun holster, German shepherd."

"Those aren't German shepherds. They're Alsatians," Benny says and ducks down in his seat as another group comes by. They all have guns. The barking dogs are pulling at their leashes.

"I give up," I say.

"It's Gemima, of course."

"You cheated. Proper names aren't allowed, are they, Mrs Schaumbacher?"

166

"Let's see if we can play the Quiet Game for a while. The first one to make a noise loses." Mrs Schaumbacher rubs her temple with the tips of her fingers.

Benny and I don't say a word, and then I make a sign for Ching-Chong-Cha. You can play it without making a peep. Benny beats me three times in a row. His favourite is rock. Mine is scissors. We hardly ever do paper. I point at him, it's the start of a new round. I wait a second. As soon as I see his fingers are about to make scissors, I quickly make my fist into a rock. I use this trick until I've got more points than him.

Benny gets it, and shouts: "Cheat, cheat, cheat! You're not allowed to wait like that, you must show as soon as I do!"

"You lose, Scumbucket." I tap Mrs Schaumbacher on the shoulder. "I won, didn't I? He was the first to break silence."

She leans over the seat, her forehead full of creases. "Yes, Margaret, you win." Then she says: "Gemima, I'm afraid I have to leave you all in the car for a while. My friend doesn't seem to be coming."

She gets out and opens the boot. "Oh no, this is all I need." She comes around to the side of the car. "The handle on one of the baskets is broken. Benny, I'm going to need you to help me carry it."

Gemima offers, but Mrs Schaumbacher says it's best if she stays put with me in the car. "Don't move," she says, and wags a red fingernail at me.

Gemima and I sit waiting in the car. She gives me a turn at the embroidery, but clicks her tongue and takes it back. "Some people aren't made to embroider. You're not like your sister, maybe you'll learn to sew with a machine like your mummy."

I look out of the window. I bet Benny's having all the fun without me. I tell Gemima I need to take a walk and stretch my legs. "I'm getting a deep vein thrombosis," I say, but she tells me to sit still and stop fidgeting.

"Read your new book. The time will pass quick-quick."

I'm too hot to read. Benny's probably having an ice cream. I climb over to the front of the car and search the glovebox for something to play with. I find a roll of stale mint humbugs and a map book. I slip my hand down the sides of the seats – but there isn't a single coin. Not even an old tickey.

"The car's too hot," I say. "The seats are scorching my legs. I'm getting third-degree burns in here."

Gemima rolls all the windows down but it makes no difference. I touch the steering wheel and it hurts my fingers. Benny will never let me forget he had the best time while I just had to sit in a stinking hot car.

Now I've got a real excuse. "I really have to go. I'm going to wet myself if I don't."

Gemima grabs my arm. "Don't you dare! Think about something else."

"Fine, I'll just do my business by the side of the car."

"No! Get out, just get out of the car. We'll find somewhere nearby."

Gemima holds my hand as we walk down the pavement, dodging a policeman and his dog. We pass the statue of Paul Kruger, the old Afrikaner who wears a hat exactly like Scrooge

McDuck's. In front of us is a crowd of Africans who look smart in their church clothes, and there are lots wearing green and black. Green's my least favourite colour after yellow, but I like black, it's Lucy's favourite. My mother says I'm too young to wear it. I also spot an Indian in a sari with a red spot on her forehead. "Look, look there," I say to Gemima when I see an African in a long white skirt with lots of beaded necklaces around her throat. "Look, she's wearing a folded serviette on her head! It's exactly like one of your pretty swans, Mima!"

We're all standing across the road from a fancy building. Gemima tells me it's the Palace of Justice. It's a funny-looking palace because there's no tower. She squeezes my hand as we squash through the crowd. I hope there's a toilet somewhere.

The palm trees don't shade us from the sun. Photographers fill every inch of the palace steps. Their cameras flash as a big army truck comes to a stop in front of us before it drives off again.

It begins to rain. Just a few drops, but it gets harder and umbrellas pop open. My hair is stuck to my forehead and someone holds a newspaper over my head. Most people start moving away, but some stay and start singing. They're holding their arms up in the air. I ask Gemima why they point their thumbs upwards, but she doesn't hear me.

Some cars drive past, and there are lorries with policemen standing up in them, and more police vans too. A big black van comes along; it's in the middle of the line of cars, and when the people see it they sing louder. But it turns the corner and disappears. The policemen in front of the palace touch the guns at their belts. They don't smile, and they don't frown either. They just stand there in their smart khaki uniforms, watching us.

"Mayibuye," a man shouts, and then there's a roar like a lion: "iAfrica." I join in, as they all keep saying these words, over and over again. Africa, Africa, that's where I live! I jump about in the rain, holding both my hands in the air, with my thumbs sticking out. Gemima's fingers bite into my arm as she says, "Thula, wena!" It's such fun, so I ignore her.

An African walks down the palace stairs. She's wearing a big black hat, it's not a crown, but it makes her look like a queen. I wave at her, but Gemima slaps my hand down.

The people shout, "Winnie! Winnie!"

She turns to the crowd and puts her hand up. She's made a fist, I wonder why? Then she shouts out loud: "Amandla!"

The people shout back: "Ngawethu!"

Power. It is ours. I feel wonderful, and my bladder is about to burst.

Policemen come closer, and their dogs are barking and there's spit on their teeth. People in front of me start to scream, and I lose my balance and fall on the ground. I cover my head with my arms, there are feet and legs all around me.

Gemima pulls me up and drags me away, her hands under my armpits. We push through the crowds, down a side street.

At last we find a lavatory. I go inside the *Europeans Only/Slegs Blankes* entrance. There's no toilet paper and I squat over the bowl, careful not to touch the seat. My mother says public toilets are dirty. Gemima stands outside on the pavement, and then we hurry back to the car.

Benny and his mother are waiting for us. "Where on earth have you been?" Mrs Schaumbacher's face is like a beetroot. "You didn't take her into the city centre? Gemima, please tell me you didn't."

"Oh, she just took me to the toilet, Mrs Schaumbacher. We were only gone for a minute." I give her the smile of an angel, and Benny too. When I tell him where I've *really* been, he's going to kill himself.

The parking meter has expired and a piece of paper is flapping under the windscreen wiper. Mrs Schaumbacher doesn't say another word. She drives straight home and we don't stop for a milkshake at the Doll House.

The next day I have to go back to school, worse luck. I'm not feeling well because Gemima hasn't finished my apron.

She fetches the bottle of cod liver oil from the shelf in the kitchen and I open my mouth. One large spoon, with a teaspoon of molasses to take the taste away. That'll sort me out, she says.

My father is wandering around the kitchen, looking lost. "You need something, Doctor?"

"My newspaper, Ntombi. Didn't it come this morning?"

Gemima carries on doing my hair, pulling it into two pigtails. I rip out the elastics and tell her, "Higher. I want them high." My hair flies upwards towards the brush, and I watch the static.

Gemima brushes with short, hard strokes as she answers my father. "I don't see it anywhere, Doctor C-C." My scalp hurts.

My father shrugs, stubbing out his cigarette. He finishes his coffee and says, "I'll catch the news in my car on the way to work."

I fetch my blazer from the coat rack, and there it is. The *Rand Daily Mail* is stuffed behind my wellingtons. Silly Gemima! It was here all the time. I'll show it to my father when he comes home. I look inside, hunting for the cartoons. Then I see it, on page two, a photo of the palace, next to the cigarette advert. *Give a man a Lucky!* I stare at the small faces in the crowd. There I am! And Gemima's cross-patch face is right behind me. I look like a drowned rat. I can't wait to show Benny – he didn't believe me when I told him yesterday.

After school, I look for the newspaper to show Benny. But it's gone.

JENNA

"The quality of mercy is not strained. It droppeth as the gentle rain from heaven upon the place beneath. It is twice blessed ..." Palesa stands at the front of the classroom, pronouncing each word with care.

Xoliswa slams her book on the desk. "Hey, Palesa, speak normal, girl. Stop trying to be white."

The class jeers as Palesa looks up with a scowl.

"Girls! Girls! Palesa is speaking just as Portia would have in Shakespeare's time." Miss Leventhorpe looks over the top of her reading glasses and shakes her head.

"Yeah, Miss, that's my point. She doesn't have to act white. She mustn't try and be too clever."

"That's enough, Xoliswa. Please continue, Palesa, you're doing well. Let me remind you, class, we have a test on this next week."

I'm hunched over next to Soo Ling, sharing her *Merchant of Venice*. I couldn't care less about Portia or her nasty Antonio. I'm rooting for Shylock and his pound of flesh.

There's a tap-tap-tap on the intercom system, and Miss Leventhorpe holds up a finger. Palesa stops mid-sentence and lowers the book.

Could Jenna Moore please come to the principal's office. Jenna Moore, Jenna Moore, to the principal's office. Immediately, please!

The intercom signs off with a whine. The class laughs and Xoliswa says, "Hey, Jen, the principal wants ya, girl."

Screw you guys. I stand up and push the book towards Soo Ling. "Good luck," she says, her eyes glittering. The class whoops, making kissing noises behind my back as I leave.

I'm no stranger to the principal's office, but today no one's keen to cheer me up ahead of the shitstorm. The secretary is staring straight ahead at her computer screen before she whips around and points to the principal's office. Go.

I enter and close the door behind me. He flicks a finger at the chair in front of his desk. "Jenna, please sit down."

Holly is at the window. She turns as I sink to the over-stuffed seat, the back of the chair hard against my spine. I'd managed to avoid Holly this morning, but now she's got me.

"Jenna?" A smile trembles on her lips. I look down, I won't smile at her. Her face is free of make-up and her eyes are pink-rimmed, with dark pouches underneath.

"Mrs Moore, there's a chair next to your daughter, unless you feel more comfortable standing?" I look up, but Holly doesn't move. The principal picks up a pen, sets it down and shuffles some papers on his desk. "Well then, Jenna, your mother asked that I call you in. She'd like us to have a conversation about something that is troubling her. Mrs Moore?"

"Hey, *Mom.*" Holly flinches. "What's going on?" I know, of course. But if I play dumb, maybe it'll all go away.

Holly doesn't seem to know how to begin. The principal clears his throat. "It appears, Jenna, that your mother has some concerns about your behaviour towards one of our staff members. Mr Skhosana."

"Don't." Holly's voice cracks. "Just don't you dare make this about *Jenna's* behaviour. I won't stand for that."

The principal swallows, then continues: "I've spoken to the staff member concerned, and I am, at this point, satisfied." He turns to me. "But, Jenna, it seems your mother is not happy with Mr Skhosana's response."

"I won't have him spreading lies about my daughter." Holly comes over to me and squats next to my chair. "Jenna, you must know that I'll always believe you. Baby, please, tell me he didn't hurt you?"

Where did that come from? Why would she think Andile hurt me?

"Jenna, I think your mother would like to hear your side of the story. As would I." The principal leans forward, crossing his arms on the desk. "Although it does appear to me, from what I've heard, that this has been blown completely out of proportion, and is the result of some silly misunderstanding."

Some silly misunderstanding! Is that how Andile described it? Did he just laugh and throw his hands in the air: "Jenna Moore, that crazy girl, she's delusional."

I begin to cry, and I can't stop. How could Andile say there was nothing between us? He'd discarded me. It's like I don't matter at all to him. Everyone will despise me now. I can't bear to look up at Holly's face. She must be sneering at me, like the principal and everyone else who knows.

I grab her hand. "I just can't. I can't. Please don't make me talk about what happened. Not here. Please, Mommy."

Holly squeezes my hand. "I'm here, baby, I promise."

The principal pushes his chair back and stands up. "I don't think we should continue our discussion in my office. The school will, of course, conduct an inquiry, and at some stage Jenna will be required to make a statement."

"Don't you even think about trying to sweep this under the carpet. I swear to God, my lawyers will be on your back before the end of the day. You and your boys' club can't make this just go away."

Lawyers! Holly! As if …

The principal pulls himself erect. "I can assure you, Mrs Moore, we will leave no stone unturned to get to the truth of this matter."

"It's *Ms* Moore," Holly says.

"Yes, of course. Miss Moore."

She's about to react when there's a knock at the door and the secretary pokes her head in. "Excuse me for interrupting, I've been asked to fetch Jenna Moore. The bus is waiting."

Behind her is Soo Ling, who makes big eyes when she sees my wet, red face.

Piss off, Soo, just get out of here.

The principal nods. "Ah, yes. The Liliesleaf outing."

Ah, crap, I'd also forgotten about today's class trip. The school's always making us go on tours to places like the

Apartheid Museum or the Constitutional Court. They're forever shoving apartheid down our throats, as if anyone cared any more.

"You may go now, Jenna. Miss Moore, we'll be in touch." He turns and calls out: "Soo Ling, I'd like a quick word with you. The bus can wait."

I sit near the back of the bus with Soo Ling, ignoring the glances and whispers around me. The bus pulls off and music blares. Girls strut down the aisle, dancing to the beat.

I lean close to Soo Ling. "What did you tell him, the principal?"

"I told him what happened. How Randy Andy invited you to his flat and all. That the two of you are kind of dating. Just like you told me, Jenna." She puts her mouth to my ear and says, "On my way out, I heard him tell the secretary to call in Andy."

I close my eyes and swallow. I'm suffocating inside the bus and I can't open a window.

"You mustn't worry, I believe you. I'm on your side." Soo Ling shoots a look at Xoliswa sitting behind us because *she's* in the loop and *she* knows everything, but she's not telling. So there.

I don't look back, but I imagine Xoliswa's eyes. Two hard black balls.

The music stops but the noise doesn't. "Settle down, girls. I want to give you some background before we arrive at our destination. Girls, please!" Miss Leventhorpe lurches in the passageway as the bus swerves to avoid a taxi.

A voice from the back: "Why isn't Mr Skhosana on the bus, Miss?" Snickers and giggles. "He always takes us on these trips. Has he got a guilty conscience?"

"Mr Skhosana has other pressing matters to attend to. You'll have to make do with me. In any case, I'm familiar with this history and I have Mr Skhosana's notes."

Miss Leventhorpe adjusts her spectacles and looks at a sheet of paper. She begins to read, her voice straining to be heard.

"Liliesleaf was the farm used secretly by the African National Congress in the 1960s to plan sabotage attacks against the apartheid government. On 11 July 1963, security police raided the farm and captured members of the National High Command."

I switch off. I'm so sick of this stuff.

Miss Leventhorpe waits for the murmurs to die down, and continues. "The Rivonia trial, which ran from October 1963 to June 1964, culminated in life sentences being handed down to Nelson Mandela and seven others."

It all washes over me as I turn away to look at the traffic jam in the opposite lane. Police sirens scream as cars are diverted from the accident. The air-con in the bus battles the heat, and at last we file out.

"Are you feeling unwell, Jenna? Is there anything I can do?" Miss Leventhorpe's hand on my arm feels gentle and kind. "Do you perhaps want to talk to me about something?"

I shake my head, trying to ignore the ringing in my ears

as I follow the feet in front of me. We stop at the entrance and a sign tells us that the farm is a heritage site, with buildings restored for exhibitions. Whatever.

"Girls, I expect you all to be taking notes, Mr Skhosana will be setting a project."

"For marks, Miss? Come on, Miss, it can't be for marks?"

"Yes, Soo Ling, the project will go towards your term history mark."

I search my pockets for a pen and pretend not to hear sniping comments about sexually transmitted marks that a certain teacher will give his favourite pupil.

"Just stop this nonsense, girls! Palesa, Tebogo – yes, you two. I'm warning you." Miss Leventhorpe herds us down the Liberation Path, then comes to a sudden stop and points to the wall. "Right, all together now, let's read this quote. It's from the manifesto of Umkhonto we Sizwe, and was distributed at the start of the sabotage campaign, in December, 1961." We shuffle our feet, someone groans. When's the lunch break? "Come, girls, let's at least say the last paragraph."

I yawn, and obediently join in the sing-song recital:

"The people's patience is not endless. The time comes in the life of any nation when there remain only two choices: submit or fight. That time has now come to South Africa."

Our voices trail off and Miss Leventhorpe marches us into the complex. "There's so much to see, and we can't do it all in one short hour. So I'm quite comfortable if you split off – in pairs, mind you – and view the exhibits that interest you."

She taps her watch. "We'll meet back at the bus in precisely fifty-five minutes."

Xoliswa and Palesa mosey off to the restaurant to buy a Coke and hang around where it's cool. Other girls sit on the grass outside, listening to music on their phones. Some make a bee-line for the back of the main house, a good place for a smoke.

I follow Soo Ling past the ticket office as she heads for the auditorium. We stop in front of a short film that's flashing scenes from the trial as Mandela's voice drones from the dock. Everything is blurry black-and-white, and then the camera jumps as it shows police cars driving from the Palace of Justice. Swinging around to the crowd outside the courthouse, it zooms in on black faces and clenched fists. But there's a flash of blonde hair, a little face laughing wildly, with the furious face of a black woman trying to pull her away. Close by, police dogs tug at their leashes.

I grab Soo Ling's arm. "Did you see her? Did you?"

She raises her head from her notebook. "Who? I didn't get the judge's name – I'll have to google it."

"No, man. It's *her*, an old aunt of mine. That kid – she's the spitting image of her, I tell you. I saw a pic of her in an old family photo."

The image has disappeared, and the film comes to an end. I don't move, though. "I need to watch this again," I say to Soo Ling.

"No time. Come on, Jenna. *You* might be getting top marks from your Randy Andy, but *I* need to work hard for my marks. I'm out of here, dude."

I focus on hating Soo Ling as she marches off to one of the thatched cottages. It doesn't look anything like a place where MK High Command got up to tricks. Along the way, she drags me into a building to show me an old truck. It's really cool, so we watch the video. It's a real James Bond story, the first interesting one I've heard today. The truck transported tourists forty times – forty times! – from Mombasa to Cape Town. The idiots didn't have a clue about MK's arms and explosives stacked under the seats. And the cops never bust the carriers, either, with their false-bottomed suitcases filled with banned literature. It all got smuggled in on flights from overseas, and ended up with anti-apartheid activists.

I wander over to the next exhibit. Photos of the trialists. Mandela looks so young. And a list of names – informers, people who turned state witness, ratting on their mates, with some blatantly lying. Solitary confinement doesn't exactly sound like a holiday in Mauritius, no wonder they cracked. But how did they live with themselves afterwards? Eight people barely escaping the death sentence, given life imprisonment – and all because of *them*, and the things they'd said in court. I stare at the names, all 173 of them. What about their families, their grandkids who come here on school outings. They must feel so ashamed. Totally gutted.

A name catches my eye, the only one I can pronounce: Roger Smythers. I stare, and it hits me. That letter in Aunt C-C's filing cabinet, the one giving permission to take food to this Roger guy. Held under ninety-day detention, turned state witness. Roger the rat.

Soo Ling grabs my sleeve. "Check this out." She points to a pile of shirt collars, yellow and worn. "This is super smart: using lemon juice to smuggle messages out of prison." Sounds a bit far-fetched to me, but I saunter over. Turns out they also used special codes and invisible ink to write letters to one another from exile.

"Move along, girls, we really must get back to school." Miss Leventhorpe shoos us off in the direction of the bus.

As we arrive at the school, I see Andile's car slipping into a parking bay outside Reception. I can't face him. I slink past, trying to disappear among the rest of the group.

A cry stops me in my tracks. "It's Jenna, Mama. See, it's her." A hand folds itself in mine and I stare down into two big brown eyes, magnified under the spectacles. "You look different in your uniform, but I knew it was you. Uncle Andy came home early from school today. He sent us to pick up his homework."

Thenjiwe Skhosana looks at me and says, "So, Jenna?"

I stare down at my feet but all I can say is, "Thenjiwe."

"Yes, Andile can't be here. He's been suspended. But you know all about that, don't you?" She turns away and says, "Come, Bonni. We need to go."

I walk away, hating her for the disgust on her face. Hating myself even more.

MARGARET

Charles is lying curled up on his side in the driveway. His mouth is pulled back, like he's snarling, and his eyes are covered in slime. When I pick him up he's as stiff as Gemima's ironing board.

I put him down because there's white foam all over his mouth and I don't want to get it on my school uniform. I run inside and call my father.

"Pull yourself together, Mags. You make it sound like there's been a murder."

I take him to Charles.

"There aren't any marks on him," my father says. "I don't think he was hit by a car." He runs his hands over Charles's fur.

"Why's his mouth so gobby, Daddy?"

My father bends closer. "You didn't touch his mouth, did you, Mags?" He takes a sniff, looks at the hydrangeas. "Your mother has told Zacharias not to put down snail bait. So it can't be that. But it's definitely some kind of poison."

He calls Zacharias and tells him to bring a spade. My father says he's going inside to fetch an old sheet. When he comes back, Zacharias rolls Charles up in it.

"Under the tyre-swing tree, please Zacharias," I say. "Charles loved that tree." I show him where to dig the hole. My father goes inside again; he has to break the news to Lucy. While Zacharias shovels soil over Charles, I pick the heads off my mother's special rosebush. Her Constance Spry she brought back from England last year. I scatter the precious petals on the grave and then go inside for breakfast.

I look at my bowl of Rice Krispies, but I can't eat it. Gemima clucks and fusses. "How about I make some French toast with syrup?" I shake my head. I don't open my mouth in case I bawl my eyes out. Cry baby, cry.

I don't know why I'm so sad. I think it's because I feel guilty that I never loved Charles enough. I keep remembering the horrible things I did to him. The time I locked him out of the house in winter after he made a wee on my school suitcase. The night I kicked him off my bed, he was too heavy on my feet.

"Cheer up," my father says. "Remember all the good times you had with Charles." He kisses the top of my head as he leaves for work. "He was a happy cat. You and Lucy loved him a lot."

I think of the times I used to cover my finger with Pecks and let Charles lick it off, his tongue like sandpaper on my skin. The summer holiday I put him on a surfboard and pulled him around the Schaumbachers' swimming pool. Charles wasn't a normal cat, he loved water, I know he did. Thinking about the good times with Charles makes me feel even worse, because there were so few of them.

I wish I knew for sure Charles had gone somewhere with lots of leather couches to wee on and where people didn't smack him when he clawed the furniture.

An upstairs door slams and I hear Lucy shout, "Those yellow-bellied snakes! They didn't have to kill my cat."

"Oh, don't be so dramatic." Now it's my mother's voice. "Rather blame the Rademeyers' garden boy and his snail bait."

Lucy comes down and marches into the kitchen. Her face is pale, her mouth tight. "Where did Zacharias put him?"

I take her outside and show her the petals decorating the grave. She puts her arm around my shoulders and pulls me close. I squeeze her tight and think about asking my mother for a kitten for Christmas.

Lucy doesn't cry as she bends down. "I'm sorry, Charles. I'm so sorry." She says it as if she's to blame.

Gemima walks me to school. I don't feel like talking. At the gate, she takes a coin from her purse and says, "This is specially for you. Buy something sweet from Tickey Sister." I feel a lot better.

Benny doesn't do catechism with the rest of the class. When he started at our school this year his father wrote a letter to Mother Superior asking for an exemption from religious instruction. During assembly, he and a couple of other Jewish children wait outside the hall until we've finished the prayer and the hymn. Afterwards, they come back inside for announcements.

Benny's a lucky fish he doesn't have catechism. Sister Columbanus is a tyrant, we have to know the books of the New Testament off by heart: Matthew, Mark, Luke and John, the Acts of the Apostles following on, all the way to the three Johns, Jude and Revelation. Sister Columbanus doesn't bother too much with the Old Testament because that's what the Jews believe.

Sometimes Benny has to sit at the back of the class and write essays on religious topics Sister Columbanus sets him – Judas Iscariot and the role the Jews played in the death of Our Lord. The penguins also give him chores to do, like washing the desks or the sports lockers. He never gets to fill the ink wells or sharpen the pencils with the big sharpener on the teacher's desk. Those jobs are a special privilege.

Today Sister Columbanus is teaching us about hell. It's the place children go if they commit a mortal sin. So I try to remember to wear a vest, and not to pick my nose, and especially to wash my hands after going to the lavatory. Hell is where sinners go if they die without receiving the last rites. The others go to heaven. And some go to purgatory.

I think about Charles, and how he clawed my mother's Sanderson couch in her special lounge. And made a wee on my father's doctor bag. I'm sure Charles didn't repent. But he never caught birds. So I don't think God would be so mean as to keep him out of heaven. No, he just couldn't.

I put my hand up. Sister Columbanus's eyes go squiff. She doesn't like us asking questions, especially not me.

"Where do cats go when they die?" I ask. "The good ones."

"Cats don't have souls. No animals do. When they die they can't go to heaven. It's only for Catholics who have repented and had their sins forgiven."

I feel sick for Charles. And for Gemima. She isn't a Catholic. Nor is Sophie, or lots of their Methodist friends. I know they believe in Our Lord. At Christmas time my mother lets Gemima have her church party in our garage. They sing hymns the whole morning and eat chicken and potato salad, which my father pays for. Sometimes Mrs Rademeyer complains the natives are making one hell of a balloo and they must thula.

"What about Africans, Sister? Where do they go?"

Sister Columbanus's mouth twitches. "Natives are human beings and also have souls." She looks daggers at me. "So, they must of course go to heaven. Just like us."

Louise Daincroft waves her hand in the air. Me. Me. Me. "But will we all live together in the same place?"

Sister Columbanus picks up a pencil and scratches her head. It must get terribly hot under that doek. "There are many rooms in our father's mansion, and there is a place for everyone. Including the African."

"No way, my father wouldn't let our garden boy sleep in the same house as me and my sister. Maybe the natives sleep outside in the back rooms of the mansion." Louise Daincroft nudges me in the ribs; she thinks she'll get a gold star for that solution.

"Natives are dirty. They smell." A boy in front holds his nose as though someone has made a poep. Another voice pipes up, "If you sleep in the same house you'll catch a disease from them and die."

There's a laugh from the back of the class, and Benny shouts out, "That's stupid. You'd already be dead if you were in heaven."

Sister Columbanus grabs her ruler. "You said something, Mr Smart Alec Schaumbacher?"

Benny puts his head down, then he looks up and says: "I just don't think Africans are dirty. That's all. You can't die from being near them."

Sister Columbanus stares at Benny like he's played a record backwards to hear Satan's message. "Come to the front of the class."

Poor Benny. His legs have only just recovered. I even helped him pick his scabs. I jump up and say, "It's true! You can ask my father. He's slept *two* nights in my Mima's room and *he* never got sick. You can ask him yourself. He knows, he's a doctor."

"Sit down, Margaret. It's most unseemly for you to comment on your parents' sleeping arrangements."

The class laughs like a bunch of monkeys in the Johannesburg Zoo.

I roll my eyes. They didn't hear me properly. "No, sillies, not my *mother's* room. My father slept with my *nanny* for two whole nights. In her room. Her name's Gemima, but I call her Mima."

Sister Columbanus has forgotten all about beating Benny. She tells us to get on with colouring in our picture of Jesus raising Lazarus from the dead. She needs to see Mother Superior very urgently.

I colour Lazarus orange because Louise won't lend me the pink crayon from the Faber-Castell set she got for her birthday. Sister Columbanus makes Louise keep them in her suitcase because last week two pencils went missing and she doesn't want Louise's crayons to provoke another occasion of sin.

The courtyard bell rings loudly. Sister Columbanus is calling Mother Superior from her quarters. The convent has a strict rule of silence. The penguins aren't allowed to run around screaming like banshees.

JENNA

"I know it's not raining, baby, but I'm still taking you to school, okay?" Holly's lips are set in a pale line. No lipstick.

She's up early this morning, sipping a cup of coffee, her hair scraped back in a ponytail. The kitchen table is stacked with cereal boxes, and there's a milk jug instead of the usual no-name longlife box. There's even some fruit.

From the scullery comes the noise of the washing machine battling with a load. I also noticed a bunch of irises in the hallway.

This whole Andile saga has flipped Holly completely. She's obviously drowning in guilt. She thinks she's failed me, ruined my life through neglect, leaving me vulnerable to a predator teacher. She's trying to compensate for fifteen years of bad mothering.

A month ago, I'd have been blown away by these changes. Maybe a little untrusting, not sure whether the new Holly wasn't as superficial as her latest shade of nail polish. I'd have given her a chance, at least. But now it feels like it's all too late. Between us, we've messed everything up and I can't see how it can be fixed. There've been too many lies.

I make a cup of rooibos and shake my head as Holly hands

me the box of bran flakes. "I'm not hungry. And I'd rather walk to school. I need fresh air." I wasn't planning on going to school today, not after yesterday.

The news of Andile's suspension had spread over the weekend like herpes at the matric rage, and no one wanted to have anything to do with me. At break, groups stood around whispering in the quad. As soon as I came near, they turned their backs and shut up. Xoliswa's afro floated like a cloud between us.

"Xols. Hey, Xols," I called. She didn't answer. I skulked off, and hid in the toilet for the rest of the day. By the time I left school, my face was stiff and sore from not crying.

As for the teachers, they looked over my head in class, and not one of them made eye contact with me. Being the focus of teachers' attention had never been high on my list, but being treated like I didn't exist was awkward and horrible.

Soo Ling was the only one still talking to me. She had to – we shared a desk. She was probably aiming to tweet about her trauma later. So I stopped talking to her. I wasn't going to become fodder for her attention-seeking on Twitter.

I couldn't face this again today, and tried to ignore Holly's voice. "Come, Jenna. Get your blazer and bag. I'm driving you to school." Can't she just leave me alone? She's probably read the troll comments on my Facebook page, all the filthy garbage. If only I'd killed my account immediately.

Holly was targeted by the trolls too, but came out fighting: I will not be intimidated. I will take whatever steps available to me to protect my daughter against abuse.

The last thing I did on Facebook was to check Andile. But he wasn't there. And he's left Twitter too.

As we turn into the school driveway Holly swears under her breath. I glance up and see a row of girls lining the gravel road, holding up big white placards. I feel a prickle of sweat as I read: *We stand by our teacher.* And: *Down with white lies!*

"Typical. Throwing the race card at us to cover up for what he's done. Well, I won't have them calling you a liar." As we drive past, Holly swears again. "Isn't that Xoliswa? Is that *our* Xoliswa who's spent more days in *my* home than in her own? What the hell does she think she's playing at?"

"Please, just drive," I say. "Don't make a scene."

She parks the car outside Reception and turns to me. "Listen, baby, I don't like this one bit. I think we need to make another plan."

"What do you mean?"

"This school inquiry isn't going to get you any justice. Not if this kind of crap is allowed to go on. We have to get the police involved. The school board will be forced to take this seriously as soon as we lay a criminal charge." She starts the car and slams the gear into reverse.

"No, wait. I can't. Please, Holly. Don't make me do this."

She looks at me, her eyes filling with tears. "Jenna, darling, I'll support you all the way. You're not alone."

I grab my satchel and fling open the door. "I can't. It's too horrible. I won't do it," I say. "And now I *have* to go to school." I slam the door shut and stalk off, then I watch as she speeds off down the driveway. The protesters jump back, and one drops her placard.

Once Holly has disappeared, I keep my head down and trot off to the school gate. Comments are tossed at my back: "Lying skank!" and "White bitch!"

I have to get away, I can't let Holly drag me off to the police station. The last thing I wanted was for Andile to get into trouble. I kept quiet about it all, but it hasn't gone away. Shit just got real.

MARGARET

Gemima is going home to the farm for her annual two-week holiday. She's changed into her travelling clothes and her hair is tucked under a navy-blue beret. My mother's skirt looks pretty on her. It's almost new, but my mother said the pleats make her hips look too big, so the girl can have it. Gemima is taller and thinner than my mother. A real skinny malinky long legs.

Gemima's face shines with Vaseline and, instead of her black lace-ups, she's wearing her church shoes. "You look beautiful, Mima. Just like a white madam." I press my face into her soft tummy and she doesn't push me away or complain that I'll crease her skirt. She just hugs me even harder. I smell her special going-out perfume. Like lucky-packet sweets.

"Try not to get into too much trouble. And be a good girl for your mummy," she says to me.

My father is taking Gemima to Park Station so she can catch the train to Durban. Someone from the farm will meet her at the other side and give her a lift. It's about a hundred miles to the sugar plantation where her family lives. My father lived there before he went to the University of the

Witwatersrand to study to be a doctor, and then my Uncle Frank took care of the farm.

Gemima is taking her holiday early because we aren't spending Christmas with Uncle Frank this year. He'll be eating turkey with his scheming minx and her old Natal family in Pietermaritzburg, where there's a hospital for her baby. I'll soon have a baby cousin. I can't wait. My father says we'll have Christmas at home and do Carols by Candlelight at Zoo Lake. Yippee, yippee, yay-yay!

Gemima has packed for Africa, and her boxes are chock-a-block. There are the striped curtains from my father's study and the clothes I've outgrown for the children on the farm. Lucy donated some old toys, but I was a bit sad when she gave away her paper dolls with all their pretty dresses. Lucy told me that the children on the farm didn't have much, so I mustn't be selfish.

The Chevy is filled with boxes and boxes of our old stuff that Gemima's been collecting all year. Her family will be happy to get these presents from her. The boxes fill the boot and the back seat, so Gemima has to sit in front with my father. She has tucked her purse with the train ticket into her bosom. My father gives her an envelope for her mother, and she tucks this in too. "An early Christmas box. Tell you mother she must only spend it on herself."

Yesterday I heard my mother say, "Really, darling, you shouldn't spoil her. She'll only take advantage."

My father is late for supper and in a foul mood after dropping Gemima off at the station. I hear him say forbidden words in

195

the hallway. "Those bloody hairybacks. They gave us the third degree."

I follow my mother to greet him, and she stands there, slapping her skirt with an oven glove. "But why didn't you take Lucy with you? It's always best to have a white woman in the car. They don't stop you then. I've told you this."

"They were bloody unreasonable. They pulled us off the road, treated us like criminals and refused to let us go. I told them who I was and where we lived but they seemed to know that already. Ntombi nearly missed her train. Bunch of Dutchmen."

"Yes, it's ridiculous they suspected you of breaking their distasteful law. But please, let's not allow them to completely ruin our supper."

JENNA

I'm left standing on the pavement a good ten minutes before Aunt C-C lets me in. She's not exactly leaping over the moon at the prospect of my company.

"Are you skipping school again today? Let me guess, it's a religious holiday." She's dressed for best. Pantyhose, shoes with heels, buffed to a shine – and a belted dress that shows how much weight she's lost in the two weeks I've known her.

I don't answer, my heart's not in it, telling more lies. A bleak mass the size of the Sahara has colonised my chest. My eyes prickle. I look down. I don't want her to see my ugly, about-to-cry face.

"I'm not feeling so good. I can't go to school. Please, I just want a space to be quiet." There's an ache in my throat, as if I'd swallowed a boiled sweet down the wrong way.

"If you're feeling unwell you should go to the doctor and get a tonic. I have a very important meeting this morning and I can't be dealing with any aggravation."

I don't move. She finally caves and lets me inside, her hand making awkward patting gestures on my arm. "Oh, very well, but I don't want to hear a peep from you," she says quickly, her face pale and strained.

"I promise, I'll just pack boxes. You won't even know I'm here."

Aunt C-C has set a tray for tea in the front room, but I follow her to the kitchen where she waits for the kettle to boil. She looks at her watch, at the clock on the wall, at her watch again. She's beyond agitated, like a four-year-old with ants in her pants. Then she's up and down the passage, straightening pictures, hands hovering over surfaces, touching, fiddling, faffing.

A VIP is coming to tea, the granddaughter of someone she'd known growing up in Joburg. That's all the info she's sharing.

At the sound of hooting outside the house, she frowns. "For heaven's sake, I did warn her about the broken buzzer and told her to telephone when she arrived." She taps her watch. "And just look at the time! I was expecting her half an hour ago." With a flap of her hand, she says, "Go on! Upstairs with you, now."

I reach for the kettle and she gives a strangled cry. "No, leave it. I can manage." The impatient cretin outside has a hand stuck to the hooter. As I leave, I hear a cracked voice behind me. "This scarf isn't too loud, is it?"

She's patting her head, fiddling with the knot at her neck.

"Loud? It's screaming hysterically."

Aunt C-C's eyes are huge, she's really uptight. I tuck her shirt label inside her collar and give her shoulder a pat. "Sorry, Aunty, I was being flippant. You look very dignified. Just perfect."

She pinches her cheeks and totters towards the front door to greet her guest. I go off in the direction of the spare room, but at the top of the stairs I stop and wait.

A woman's voice floats up as the front door opens. "Fana, wait outside with the car. This neighbourhood is no good."

"Your driver is more than welcome to come inside. There's a trustworthy security guard, he'll take care of your car." Aunt C-C's voice seems unusually shaky.

"No, he must wait outside." A murmur, and the front door slams shut. "I usually have people come to my office. I am not in the habit of doing this, but Comrade Harry said I should make an exception in your case."

"Do you always listen to Comrade Harry?" Aunt C-C drawls. She's clearly back on form. Then she says, "Harry's a dear friend, we know each other from exile days in London."

"Yes, I know about you whites, running away and living it up on the French Riviera, leaving us behind to fight the boers."

"Well, that's one point of view, of course. OR always advised me to only take holidays in Brighton. He said it'd be sure to rain there, and I'd be suitably miserable."

"That Oliver Tambo! Yes, I've heard he had a good sense of humour." The woman laughs. "Harry mentioned I might find what you say interesting. But I'm afraid I don't have much time for interesting."

"Do you at least have time for tea? Your grandmother always had a cup at this time of the morning. I'm an Earl Grey person myself, I can't stand that rooibos nonsense."

"So, you knew my grandmother. Is that what this is about?"

"I knew Gemima."

"I don't think she's known by that name. Her name was Ntombifuthi Ndlovu. I've taken her surname – my mother never married, you see."

"I've never forgotten her name," Aunt C-C says, her voice softening. Then briskly, she says, "I've set a tray for tea in the front room. Just a minute while I fill the teapot." Her footsteps echo along the passage and a few moments later there's loud coughing. It sounds like she's shredding her lungs. Then, "Please come along, there are a few things I want to show you, and I have much to tell you. I hope you'll bear with me." The hacking cough again. "It's been over fifty years, and I don't think I can keep quiet any longer."

Their voices fade as they head for the front room. I sit at the top of the stairs, straining my ears, but Aunt C-C has shut the door. I stay put, and a few minutes later a door opens. There's a noise in the passageway, and then Aunt C-C shuffles off to the front room again. This time, she leaves the door open, and I climb down a step or two.

"I kept all these letters. They're from your great-grandmother to Gemima, written over the period she worked for us. I'm afraid your mother never wrote to Gemima. You know, of course, that she left the farm before you were born. No one ever heard from her again." Aunt C-C's voice falters. "I have some photographs too. Not many, but I've made an album which you must have."

"My mother was a city girl, she was not a good daughter,

and my childhood was …" The door to the front room closes, and there's silence. Eventually, I wander off upstairs to see what mess I can clear away into boxes. On my way to the spare room, I pass Aunt C-C's bedroom. The bed's been made, but the rest of the room is a tip. Boxes are stacked on the floor, and papers are spread out on a dressing table. On the nightstand I notice a child's handwriting on a sheet of paper and read:

> For Charles (by Margaret Beatrice
> Channing-Court)
> Charles, you were the prince of cats
> Even though you drove my mother bats
> Rest in peace, Charles my dear,
> I won't forget you, never fear.

At the sound of voices, I quietly leave. I stop for a while at the top of the stairs, and as I look down at the passage below, the woman says: "So many casualties from that terrible period, isn't it time to forgive yourself?"

Forgive. To forgive Holly for her lies. And myself for what I've done to Andile. He'll never forgive me, of course. He shouldn't.

Aunt C-C looks up and catches sight of me. "Jenny? What on earth do you want?"

I come down, and though Aunt C-C's eyes are puffy and pink, she manages to throw me a black look. I ignore her, reach out my hand to the woman. "I'm Jenna Moore."

She puts down the album she's carrying and says, "Hello, Jenna, I'm Thabisa Ndlovu." She turns to Aunt C-C. "Your granddaughter?"

Aunt C-C cocks her head at me. "She's not really mine, but I suppose I might think of her in that way. Jenny, Miss Ndlovu is a Supreme Court judge."

Am I expected to kiss her hand or something? I shake it instead. Heavy with gold rings, her hand lies limp in mine. The two of them walk to the front door, and I follow them to the car.

The judge waits for her driver to open the door and settles into the back of the black BMW. "Thank you for making contact. I know how hard it must have been for you. I'll pass on your greetings to Harry."

The car accelerates, slows to avoid a pothole, and we turn back to the house. Aunt C-C pulls the gate shut. Inside the house, she rests her hand on my shoulder and sags like a pap balloon. "Jenny, my dear, I have to lie down, and you must go home. I need to be alone." She staggers towards the stairs, holds on to the bannister and huffs as she climbs.

"Before I go, can I bring you something? You want some more tea?"

She pauses, turns around. "That would be nice." She smiles at me. "Don't forget to warm the teapot."

MARGARET

My mother and I are going shopping in town to buy a wedding anniversary present for my father. Tomorrow they will celebrate a fifth of a century of married bliss, apart from one or two small disappointments. It's their China anniversary. Ching-chong-Chinaman!

We don't often shop in town; it makes my mother nervous. She only ever goes out to buy fabric and patterns from Fairplays and to have her hair done once a week at a salon a short drive from our house. We never shop for clothes because my mother makes mine, but she's promised I can have a dress from the OK Bazaars when I turn ten in three months' time. I can't wait for February.

My mother doesn't like driving the Chevy into town, so we must take the number 14 Sydenham trolley bus off Louis Botha Avenue. Two buses packed with Africans drive past, and then ours arrives. I race upstairs past the sign: *Moenie Spoeg Nie!* I find a seat at the front so I can get a decent view. We drive off, the purple jacaranda branches walloping the roof along the way.

The bus conductor comes round to collect our money and give us our tickets and change. The coins come from tubes in the money belt around his waist. Benny says when he's big he wants to be a klippie so he can also wear one. I don't think he'll be allowed because he's not an Afrikaner.

My mother lets me ring the bell before our stop. We hop off near the Loveday Street terminus, and walk to John Orr's.

"First floor, ladies' lingerie," the lift boy calls out, first in English, then Afrikaans. "Household goods, second floor." The metal gates open, then clang shut. At last – the fourth floor. "Menswear."

I help my mother choose a blue-and-white striped shirt and a pair of cuff links. And now, time for tea on the top floor.

It's heavenly. Cucumber sandwiches on white bread with the crusts cut off so I don't have to hide them under a serviette, and scones with cream and strawberry jam. My mother complains that we're too late for the fashion show but I tell her we can still listen to the man playing the piano.

"I suppose you want a strawberry milkshake?"

"I think I'd prefer Ceylon tea, Mummy."

I'm a real lady, like my mother and all the other smart ladies. They wear white gloves, and their red lips mark the tea cups.

"Don't stare, Margaret. And elbows off the table. And don't slurp."

My mother nods her head when someone she knows passes our table. "Good morning, Mrs Guthrie." Then she dabs her lips and gives a smile, showing her teeth. "Yes, I don't often come into town, but I'm shopping for my husband's anniversary present. Twenty blissful years."

As Mrs Guthrie moves away, I say under my breath, "Spastic colon."

I know interesting things about some of the ladies in the room. My father lets me help him file his patient records for when he does his home visits. They're in his study cabinet.

"Varicose veins," I mutter as Mrs Desmond hurries away from our table.

The ladies don't chat much. They nod, then edge away. "They normally like to talk the hind leg off a donkey." My mother sounds cross, even though she says social intercourse makes her nervous. She holds her finger in the air, calling for the bill.

We wait, service isn't what it was, according to my mother. Mrs Bradley, who has troublesome tonsils, comes up to our table. My mother and Mrs Bradley chat, although my mother keeps trying to end the conversation: "Well, lovely seeing you," she says, and "Do give my best regards to your sister."

My mother isn't terribly fond of Mrs Bradley. I once heard her telling my father that she was a vicious gossip and drank cocktails before midday. Her daughter, Eleanor, is in my class at school. She wears her hair in a long white plait, like Rapunzel.

"Do you still have that girl working for you?" Mrs Bradley pulls out a chair and sits down with us. "Gemima, I think you call her."

"Yes, of course. Gemima is one of the family. My husband

brought her from the farm a couple of months after Lucy was born. My children adore her." My mother opens her compact and fixes her lipstick. "And she's not at all cheeky and is awfully clever with stains. Why? Are you looking for someone?"

Mrs Bradley pulls her mouth down. "Well, we have our Lizzie. Sixty years old and still jolly capable. Safe, too. Although of course I'd still feel perfectly safe even if Lizzie was younger." She widens her eyes at my mother. "Some of our men have a fiendish appetite for chocolate, if you get my meaning."

My mother clears her throat and glances at me. "Yes, it is regrettable."

"Daddy and I both love chocolate," I say.

"Quiet, Margaret." My mother wiggles her finger in the air; the bill still hasn't arrived.

Mrs Bradley lowers her voice as my mother puts some banknotes down on the plate. "I'm always at the other end of a telephone if you need me. You can trust me to be discreet." Her eyes glint.

We get up from the table and stop off at the first floor. My mother buys a pair of nylons, and silk gloves to match her anniversary dress. The gloves are the wrong shade of blue. I tell my mother this, but she says they will just have to do.

"I suppose you could give them to Mima when she comes back from holiday," I say.

My mother says that will be the day.

Today is my parents' anniversary, and my father serves my mother tea and a boiled egg in bed. I've arranged yellow roses in my grandmother's precious vase, and placed it at my mother's bedside. Roses aren't the traditional China wedding anniversary flower, my father said, but he couldn't find any asters or day lilies.

I've hidden a small box, wrapped in silver paper, on the tray. It's under the tea cosy, so my mother can't see it. We got it from Katz & Lurie, where my father buys all her jewellery.

My mother sips her tea and I try to keep my face straight. I don't look at the tray. Then my father winks at me, and I slide my hand under the tea cosy and hold out the box.

"Open it, look inside!" I bounce on the end of the bed and say, "Look, look, look!"

"Stop that, Margaret," says my mother. She opens the box and lifts out the silver locket. I'd helped my father put the tiny photos of Lucy and me inside it.

"My two daughters. Only two." My mother's lips tremble as she examines the photos. She looks up at me and says, "This was taken when you started growing your hair. See, rats' tails. But at least Lucy isn't wearing that ghastly beret."

"Can I, please, Mummy? Can I fasten it for you?" I jump off the bed and go to her.

"Perhaps another day," she says and puts the locket back on the velvet in the box. She looks at my father, her eyes filling with tears.

He sighs. "I'm sorry, darling. I'm a complete idiot. I didn't think."

JENNA

I turn off the light and watch as the branches outside my bedroom window claw at the ceiling with their shadows.

Holly knocks, then comes in. I breathe in and then out again, pretending to sleep. My eyes are half open, but I don't want to talk to her.

She sits on the end of my bed with her head bowed. I turn on my side, my back to her, making a soft snoring noise. I can't stand the pressure she's putting on me. Too many questions I don't want to answer. Please, Holly, go away.

"I know you're awake, Jenna. I'm not going to turn on the light, or make you speak to me. But I've got something to tell you." Holly crosses her legs on the bed, tucking her feet underneath her.

"You've asked me about your dad, and it's time I told you. I'd prefer not to. But I think it's important that you know, especially now that you're dealing with this incident with your teacher, and refuse to talk to me about it."

I turn onto my back so that I can see her face in the light from the street. Shoot, Holly, I'm listening.

"You know of course that when my parents died in a car crash I was sent to live with Aunt C-C at her house in

Pembroke Street." She's picking at her nail polish again, I know. "Coming from Durban, everything was strange to me: Joburg was terrifying, and I had to deal with a cranky old aunt I'd never met before. I was only fourteen, I hated my new school, and I wasn't coping with losing my mom and dad."

The phone rings in the passage and Holly falls silent till it stops. It rings again, but she makes no move to get up and answer it.

"Aunt C-C tried her best, I suppose. She came back from London a few years after Mandela's release. She was all fired up about helping to build the New South Africa. Too busy to bother about me." Holly puts her elbows on her knees and leans towards me. "See, Jenna, I guess I was a bit of a disappointment. I really didn't give a toss about all the stuff she was into."

My pillow feels hot under my head. I flip it over and lie back on the cool cotton cover. "You were going to tell me about my father. I don't want to know all this boring history between you and Aunt C-C."

"I was a rebel at school, but I've already told you this." She chuckles. "Maybe it was a reaction against Aunt-C-C. She disapproved of my friends and everything I said or did. I was totally boy-mad, and in my matric year I started going steady with Danny."

Danny-boy. At last. We're getting to my father. He's dead, but I still want to know about him.

"Aunt C-C couldn't stand him. I don't blame her. Danny was rotten. You know I always go for the bad boys."

"Lots of girls date bad boys," I say. "Don't you think it's a bit late to start beating yourself up about it?"

"Fine, thanks for that. So, anyhow, a few weeks into my first year at university, Danny and I went to a party. By this time, I'd been fully sucked into his druggie lifestyle."

I can hear her picking at her nail polish again, then she chews and spits. "Do you need to be doing that?" I say. "It's really disgusting"

"Sorry," she says. "Talking about drugs and Danny makes me edgy, you see." She folds her hands, wringing them. "I'm going to keep this part short, Jenna, I'm not proud of it, okay? I was into experimenting, doing anything Danny gave me. Smoking, sniffing, popping tabs. Drinking a lot too."

She reaches for the glass on my bedside table, and takes a long sip of water. "We ended up in The Wilds. You know that nature reserve off Houghton Drive? Parts of it are closed off to the public now, but in my day it was a place where kids hung out and partied. There was a whole crowd of us, tripping, completely off our heads."

Holly's phone rings. She flinches, takes it out of her pocket and silences it. She's clearly not bothered about clients or tomorrow's show days; they can damn well wait. A gust of wind blows open the window, whipping the curtains. I pull the duvet up around my shoulders.

Holly shuts the window and curls up at the end of my bed, hugging my feet. "The party really got going. Someone had a ghetto blaster, we were dancing, drinking – and smoking weed, of course. Couples were making out, the usual stuff. One of the guys passed around some tabs. Some girl started hitting on Danny. We were supposed to be together but he was more interested in the other chick. I was pissed off and we had a row. He told me to take my bad attitude and get lost."

My feet feel hot. I push Holly away, kick open the duvet. "So, did you?" I say. "Did you get lost?"

"At some point I went for a walk. I needed to pee, and to cool down. Maybe smoke a joint and come down a bit from the tabs. They'd really messed up my head. I squatted behind a bush, and on my way back, I bumped into a group of guys smoking weed around a fire. I joined them, and one of the guys started getting fresh with me. It made me feel good, I was still hacked off with Danny about the flirty girl. Things sort of happened."

"Jeez, man, that's not cool. You were supposed to be dating Danny."

"I told you I was wasted, okay? I couldn't stop. Maybe I didn't want to. And then things got way out of hand. When we were done, he went off and I joined the other guys around the fire."

Holly clears her throat and puts a hand to the side of her face. "I carried on jolling. It got kind of wild. I woke up lying by the burnt-out fire the next morning, a dog licking my face. I couldn't find my shoes. Or my underwear."

The salmon and caper on rye that Holly had made for supper rises to my throat. "You slept with a whole bunch of guys? Are you telling me they all took advantage of you?" This sounds like something Aunt C-C might say.

Holly looks up at the ceiling, her eyes squinting at the damp in the corners, as if she was seeing it for the first time. "I don't remember if I said no. I might have had fun. I don't know."

The bed vibrates. Holly's shoulders are shaking.

"I've told myself that I was young, drunk, drugged up. I was stupid. But what kind of guy sleeps with a girl who's so far gone she probably doesn't even know her own name?"

Holly wipes her nose on the sleeve of her sweatshirt. "I won't let the same thing happen to you. When an adult sleeps with a fifteen-year-old , it's called rape. He shouldn't get away with it."

I want to tell her that Andile didn't rape me. All he'd ever been was sweet and kind. But I don't say a word, and just listen as she goes on with her story.

"When I found out I was pregnant, Aunt C-C wanted me to get rid of it. She said Danny would be a useless father, and a child deserved two parents."

"Me! You're talking about me. Not some 'it'."

"Yes, of course, baby. I knew even then you weren't just an 'it'. But I also knew you weren't Danny's." She smooths the duvet.

"Danny's not my father? Are you sure?"

"I'm sure. Danny and I were always careful. Anyway, I left Pembroke Street and wrote Aunt C-C a stinking letter accusing her of trying to make me a murderer. You know my views on abortion. It's a Catholic thing I caught from that horrible school of ours."

She twists a corner of the duvet. "I told her Danny wasn't the father of my child and that she should butt out of my business. But I couldn't tell her what had actually happened. I was too ashamed."

The letter: the one I'd found in Aunt C-C's chest of drawers, which made me set out to find my nameless, faceless father.

"Right. So, what happened to Danny, then?"

"Ag, that guy. When you were born, he wanted to be involved. We were still together, you know, in an on-off messed-up kind of way. But he just wasn't up to it. And I didn't really want him around you. He was in and out of rehab for a few years, and then the heroin did him in."

I hug my pillow, my eyes burning. The phone rings again. Ignoring it, Holly looks down at her cellphone. "Seven missed calls. Damn, it must be important. I should answer it." She goes through to the passage. "Yes? Who is this?" After a while she says, "The Linksfield hospital? I'll be right there."

Holly comes over and leans down to me. She shrugs, her arms wide open. "I have to go out now. But always remember, I love you more than all the stars in the sky." She hugs me tight, I hug her back. Harder. All the planets in the galaxy. All the galaxies in the universe.

"Who was on the phone?" I say. "Where you going?"

"Oh, it's about that old aunt of mine, C-C. One of your teachers – Miss Levenson or something – she says the old girl's in hospital. She had a fall, apparently, and has asked to see me. I guess I should go."

213

I push the duvet off and say, "I'm coming with you."

"That's sweet of you, baby, but she doesn't even know you. Stay snug in bed and I'll be back soon."

"No, I'm coming. There's something I need to tell you too."

MARGARET

Benny and his mother are leaving for Canada today. They are travelling by aeroplane, and I'm so jealous. We always drive to Durban in the Chevy when we visit Uncle Frank on the farm. But last year when I visited my grandmother and Aunty Beatrice in England, we travelled by sea, in a Union Castle Line boat. My stomach didn't agree with the tossing waves, and I spent days and days on that *Pendennis Castle* with my face over a bucket.

"I can be your pen pal in Canada, Mags," Benny says. "Sometimes I'll send you blank pages, just like Merle in Australia, so you know even though I didn't have time to write, I'm still alive and kicking."

"Don't be such a fool. Those weren't blank pages, they ..."

Benny's smiling at me, his lip curled around his top tooth. "Of course I know about writing secret letters. My mother showed me how to do it."

I don't believe him. But I just say, "Last touch, Scumbucket." I punch him and don't run away. He can have last touch.

His arms are hanging down at his side. "You got me again, Mags."

215

Benny's going to get a big surprise on the aeroplane when he opens his bag. I've put a letter and a present under his jersey. It's a bronze medal, my most precious possession. I got it a couple of years ago; it was the day we became a Republic. Lucy bunked school, and Mavis didn't go to work because her bus wasn't running. Lucky Gemima is a live-in, so she was at work bright and early, as usual. My mother cried for three days, and she didn't see our gymnastic display at the Ellis Park Stadium. These last two years she's ignored Republic Day. Instead, she's thrown a party the week before – on Empire Day. For revenge, she says.

We all got a medal to pin on our blazers, and a little flag we waved when we sang the new national anthem. I sang the loudest, ringing out from our blue heavens. Benny didn't sing at all, he just stood there. His father told him he wasn't allowed to take that ruddy medal, and when we all queued up, he hid in the lavatory so that he wouldn't be punished. I've told Benny in my letter that the medal is just a loan, it's not for ever. He has to give it back next time I see him. If he loses it, I'll strangle him to death.

I practise my cartwheels on the lawn for a while, then my mother and Lucy arrive to say goodbye to Mrs Schaumbacher and Benny. "Oh, Margaret, just look at those grass stains," my mother says.

She walks up to Mrs Schaumbacher on the stoep, and slaps the little black miggies off her legs so that they won't get itchy. Then my mother puts a nice smile on her face and says, "I do appreciate the patterns and the thread, Rachel, it was more than generous of you to send them across with Lucy." I don't understand why my mother says this, because she got awfully cross yesterday when Lucy brought the parcel over. "That woman is trying to make me feel guilty," she'd said. Gemima had to take the patterns away and put them in my doll hospital.

Mrs Schaumbacher hugs Lucy and my mother. She hugs Lucy the longest.

"Thank you for your friendship, Ellie. I'm sorry I didn't see more of you this past year," she says.

My mother's face is pink. "It's been difficult, Rachel. Things have been a bit complicated, and so forth." She twists her fingers together.

"Well, I'm glad it's over. I hope you'll write and give me news. I'm going to be so homesick."

Lucy tells Mrs Schaumbacher she'll write often, and my mother chews her lip. Gemima also arrives, and she hugs Benny and shakes Mrs Schaumbacher's hand. "Hawu, Madam, I don't know what to say." Mrs Schaumbacher has given Gemima her Singer and mountains of material so she can learn to sew her own dresses.

Gemima also gives Mrs Schaumbacher a present. She's been working on it for the last few days. Lots of handkerchiefs with tiny initials embroidered in the corners, for Mr Schaumbacher too.

The taxi hoots from the road and Mrs Schaumbacher locks the front door. She gives Lucy the keys and tells her that the estate agent will collect them later today.

Benny punches me so hard on my shoulder that I fall on the grass. "I gave Gemima something for you when I'm ten thousand feet in the sky, Mags. Don't let your mom see, she'll get cross." He runs for the car.

It doesn't really hurt, but I can't stop crying.

After they drive off, Gemima gives me a box. It's filled with Benny's comics. The whole bang shoot. I hide them under the bed in my hospital, next to the box of silkworm cocoons, and eggs that never want to hatch. I don't read the comics for a long time. They make me miss Benny too much.

I get a letter every day from Benny. He says he doesn't do much, and mostly eats hamburgers and watches television. His spelling is atrocious. I tell him he'll become obese like our dearly departed Charles, and he'll also get square eyes. I wish we had television.

Lucy's stopped getting letters from her pen pal in Canada. I suppose Monica got tired of her being such a slow coach writing back. But at least Lucy gets letters from Mrs Schaumbacher. Lucy always writes back with news from home, because my mother says she's not quite up to it. Mrs Schaumbacher uses special airmail letters, blue ones, so I don't get any stamps.

After school, I usually cycle up and down the road, playing aeroplane-aeroplane. Gemima gives me a clothes peg to clip a Bicycle card onto my wheel. As soon as I take off, the card goes phripp-phripp against the spokes. When I get to Mr Dickson's house, I'm in Australia and I eat a kangaroo. Two houses later I'm in New Zealand where I chase a sheep, Mrs Cowley's Jack Russell. I turn and cross the ocean to Canada, to Benny's house, where I hunt a big brown bear. The house is closed up, the grass is overgrown, and there's a *For Sale* sign on the pavement. It's no fun playing alone, even if I am the senior air hostess.

School is boring without Benny, and the afternoons are long. My mother says I've got an opportunity to make a nicer sort of friend. I ask Louise Daincroft to come and make coconut ice at my house with Gemima. But I hear her mother say, "With their girl, Gemima?" Then she says, "Over my dead body." Louise tells me this means no.

These days, there's another Volksie parked in the road. Not the lime-green one that was outside Benny's house. This one's pale grey. Two men with moustaches are inside. They just sit there, watching our house. Sometimes they climb into the Rademeyers' tree and peer into our back garden with binoculars. Gemima told me she's decided to take the long way round when she visits Sophie. Even when she's wearing her church shoes that pinch like the devil.

One morning, I watch Zacharias painting the garage door. My father stops to take a look. He tells him: "You'll have to give it another coat, Zacharias." He's right, Zacharias needs to cover over the ugly black writing. I can still read it: *Kaffirboetie. Sies!*

"What does it mean, Daddy?"

"Come inside, Mags, and let Zacharias finish the job. It doesn't mean anything." Then he goes off to work.

When my father gets home, I hear arguing.

"Honestly, Ellie, I haven't a clue why this nonsense has happened. They wrote something similar on the front of the Schaumbachers' house a few months ago. I expect they got our addresses mixed up."

I go into the front room, where my father is pouring himself a whisky. He finishes it, and then he pours another one. The room is awfully quiet. He says, "No, Ellie, don't look at me like that. Those people have filthy minds."

JENNA

We drive into the hospital entrance and Holly parks the car. Her hands rest on the wheel for a while and she stares straight ahead. "I'm so sorry you felt you had to go snooping around that house. When I left Pembroke Street, I took all my personal stuff. There's nothing left that could tell you anything about the four years I spent there."

We walk past the canteen filled with anxious faces huddled over tables, waiting for news. The ICU matron directs us to a ward. We disinfect our hands, put on a blue hospital cap, and search for the familiar face.

In a corner bed, her turbaned head lies back on a pillow, her eyes closed. There are tubes in her nose, and fluid drips down a tube into her arm from a bag on a stand by the bed. A monitor above her bed shows zigzagging lines of green and red.

"Aunt C-C, it's Holly."

Her eyes flicker open, she looks up and grimaces. "Well, now. Did I have to throw myself down the stairs and land myself in hospital to get you to come and see me? Really, Holly, I've been waiting for a visit for days." She gives a weak smile when she sees me. "Hello, Jenny."

"Sorry," I say. "I didn't tell Holly. I didn't want her to know I was working for you. It's a bit complicated, but now she knows about it all."

"Well, she's here now. I wonder if you could leave your mother and me alone for a few minutes? I'd like to have a private conversation with her."

"No, no more secrets," Holly says. "If you have anything to tell me, I want Jenna to hear it too." She puts her arm around me. "Jenna knows everything. All the bad stuff."

"As you choose, you know I've never won an argument with you." Aunt C-C closes her eyes and takes a deep breath. Her voice is faint, but formal, as if she is reading from a script. "I want to apologise, Holly. I failed you all those years ago when you were in my care. I should have supported you in the choice you made. I deeply regret my behaviour and the alienation between us. It was my fault." Her voice drops to a whisper as she says, "Knowing your daughter now, I wish I'd met her a long time ago."

Looking at me, Holly gives a small shrug. Then she clears her throat and says to Aunt C-C, "We both messed up. I'm sorry too, I behaved so badly. We don't have to talk about it all, it happened a long time ago. It really doesn't matter any more."

"It matters to me, Holly. I think I need to tell you why I behaved as I did, so that you'll understand. Jenny, I want you to hear this too." She grabs my hand.

"When I was young, I did something unforgiveable. Well, it was something *I* believe is utterly unforgiveable. I've

THE CHOICE BETWEEN US

regretted it all my life. I didn't want to see your life spoilt too, all because of a wrong decision. A bad choice. You see, I chose to be a person I've despised all my life. A coward." Aunt C-C begins to tell her story, her voice growing husky as tears leak from her eyes. When she eventually stops, she lies back, her eyes on the ceiling.

In the long silence that follows, her hand tightens over mine. Eventually she speaks again, her voice straining with effort: "Jenny, my dear. I don't want to stick my nose into business that doesn't concern me. But Mary Leventhorpe has told me about your trouble at school, and of course *you* concern me." She pauses, then says hoarsely: "Fifty years ago, all I needed to do was say a few simple words. It would have saved so much suffering. But I didn't have the courage." Her eyes pleading, she says, "Please, dearest girl, don't let this business with your teacher haunt *you* for the rest of your life too."

I can't bear the kindness in her voice, her eyes, as she sinks back again, her hand releasing mine. Standing next to Holly as we watch over the old woman lying peacefully before us, I feel shame wash over me. If only it could wash me clean.

A doctor passes, and then doubles back to us. "Your aunt insisted on seeing you. But I would like you to leave now, so that she can rest."

I take Aunt C-C's hand, her veins bulbous beneath the skin. "The doctor is chucking us out. He says you need your beauty sleep. So, check you tomorrow, okay?"

"Check you tomorrow, Jenny," she says with a faint smile.

I don't think she's big on hugging, so I give her hand a squeeze. Her hand clutches mine. Two pumps, almost like a heart beating.

We drive home in silence, and I try to get some sleep. It's pointless. Aunt C'C's story keeps looping in my head. I go to Holly's bedroom and stand at the door. She sees me and sits up.

"Come, I can't sleep either." Lifting her duvet, she pats the mattress.

"I can't stop thinking about what Aunt C-C said," I begin. "*She* wasn't responsible for everything that happened fifty years ago. It was a hectic time. But *I'm* to blame for my mess."

"Oh, I wish I'd known her better, Jenna. I was so stupid. But it's not too late – for either of us." Holly gives me a hug. "We'll see her tomorrow, and the day after."

It gets later and darker as we talk, and eventually there are no sounds from the street. I tell her about Andile. There is no light from the moon to expose my shame. There is no one else to hear my terrible truth. Holly listens. She holds me, and all she does is pass me loo paper till there's none left on the roll.

I open my eyes and it's still dark, even though the hadedas are screaming. But it's not the birds that have woken me. It's the phone.

I hear the door open, and then Holly murmuring in the passageway.

She doesn't have to tell me. I know.

MARGARET

It's almost bedtime and I'm brushing my teeth when I hear Gemima yelling outside. She sounds like a dustbin boy. "Aieee! Aieee!"

"It's the geyser," my father tells me as I bump into him in the passage. "It's exploded, and there's water all over the show." He's off to the garage to fetch his DIY kit. My mother discourages him from using it because she says he's a rotten handyman.

When he walks in again, he looks jolly pleased with himself. "I've managed to turn the outside geyser off, but her room's a soggy mess. Mags, help Gemima carry her things out." He says to my mother, "We can assess the damage tomorrow, and I'll call a plumber."

My father tells Gemima that she mustn't sleep in her room tonight. Her mattress is soaked like a sponge. "You can sleep with me, Mima," I say. "We can have a midnight feast."

But my mother says Gemima will be perfectly comfortable sleeping in the scullery and gives her an old blanket. "That's even more fun," I say. "It'll be like camping!"

I wake up to loud voices, and my bedroom light is switched on.

"I've told you, this is my daughter's bedroom," my father says. "Please, she's sleeping."

I sit up and blink. My father is at the door, trying to block two men. They push past him and come into my room. One has a bald head, with strands of hair combed over it. He's also got a thin moustache. The other one looks like a hungry brak. He opens my cupboard, as the bald man looks under my bed.

"Daddy, it's not time for school, is it?"

"Stay in bed, Mags. Just stay there." My father turns to the two men and says, "As you can see, it's just my daughter. Please, leave her alone."

The two men look at each other and the brak nods. My father switches off the light and closes the door. I can't go back to sleep. There's more hammering. "Unlock the door, Lucy. Please." It's my father's voice. "Make yourself decent and let me in."

I crawl out of bed and peep through a slit in the door.

"You people have a cheek. Do you hear me? Mrs Suzman will be hearing all about this and she'll raise a stink in parliament." I've never heard my mother shout so loudly.

"Please, Ellie, go downstairs and wait in the front room. I'll handle this. These gentlemen have got their facts muddled." She doesn't answer him; all I can hear is a loud sob. Then my father says, "I don't know where you chaps get your information from, but what you're suggesting is completely ludicrous."

"Where's the kaffir girl? We saw her sneak into the house last night, and she didn't leave again. We know she's here.

226

Come on, Doc, come clean with us. Show us your little love nest." The two men laugh, and I wonder what's funny.

My father doesn't laugh, he just says: "I've told you. Nothing like that is going on between my employee and me. I can't imagine why anyone who knows me would suggest such a thing."

"Just tell us where you're hiding your Bantu girl. She can tell us about the hanky-panky that's going on between you."

My father *hasn't* hidden Gemima! I run out of my room to tell them. "She's camping in the scullery. She couldn't sleep in her room tonight because it's a soggy mess. You see, the geyser burst, and my father fixed it."

"Mags, please. I told you to stay in your room." My father and Lucy are in the passage. Lucy's wearing her dressing gown, and her head's covered in pink plastic curlers.

"But Lucy's here," I say. "Why can't I?"

It's not fair.

The two men say something in Afrikaans and the brak walks off. Another man, a fat one, comes out of my parents' bedroom. His uniform is so tight around his thighs that he'll get a thrombosis. He shakes his head at the bald man. "Nothing there, and there's no evidence a native has been in the beds."

"I think it'd be best if we went downstairs and had a sensible chat about all of this." My father touches the bald man on the arm and starts moving towards the stairs.

He pushes my father's hand away. "Don't tell me what to do. We'll leave when I say so."

We wait for ages, and no one says anything. And then I

see Gemima. She's walking up the stairs in front of the brak. Her eyes are wide, her arms are wrapped around her chest. She's wearing my mother's old dressing gown, the pink one that I like. Her head looks funny without her doek.

"I found the kaffir meid," says the brak. "I also went to her room outside, and the geyser story is true. But check this out." He pulls the two other men to the side. They skinder together like old ladies after Mass, looking at a piece of paper.

"No, man. That's outside our jurisdiction. I'll get the other okes in." The bald man turns to my father and pushes the paper into his hands. "Take a look at what we found in your maid's toilet. Blerrie commie propaganda. You better get ready for a long night."

My father reads it and holds it out to him. "I've never in my life seen this leaflet. It's not mine."

"Ja, that's *your* story." He grabs my father's wrist. "But it's okay, Doc, you can keep it. There's two boxes full of inflammatory literature outside."

He takes a magazine and waves it around. "Check this one out, Doc. A book about explosives. And British coal mines, nogal. This is big trouble. Groot kak." Then he says, "Whose boxes are they?"

My father looks at Lucy. Lucy looks at Gemima. I look at Lucy, who closes her eyes.

My mother and father will scream blue murder, I know. I promised. I crossed my heart and hoped to die. I'm not going to tell on Lucy. She'll want her autograph book back, and it's *mine* now.

"We'll be calling the Special Branch," says the bald man. "They'll do a thorough search of your property." He tells us all to go downstairs, and follows us to the front room.

The rest of the night our house is like Charing Cross Station at rush hour. This is what my mother says. Men in suits come and go, they talk to the others in uniform, police vans pull up and park in the road outside. The telephone keeps ringing, and my father takes the calls.

"Just neighbours, wanting to know if everything's all right."

"Well, of course everything's not all right. Did you tell them that everything's perfectly fine?" My mother's voice is screechy.

"There's a perfectly good explanation for this. Just keep calm, Ellie." My father hands my mother a magazine, and she pages through the *Personality* without reading it. She lets me have a turn, and I do a quiz. It's about pleasing my husband. I only get three out of ten answers right because I like wearing shorts, but the right answer was "a feminine skirt". And my husband can jolly well take off his *own* shoes and socks when he comes home from work.

The whole time we're in the front room, Lucy doesn't say a word. She just smokes, lighting each new Texan with her last one, and doesn't use her Zippo at all. The only sound she makes is when she spits a bit of tobacco off her lip. Pfttt.

Gemima and I sit on the carpet. She's embroidering a nightie for Lucy's nineteenth birthday next month. Nog 'n piep! She lets me choose the colour of the thread then clicks her tongue at me, saying, "How did you get this thread so tangled? Wena!"Gemima's needle slips in and out of the fabric, doing satin stitch.

We hear the men going from room to room. First upstairs, then downstairs. My father leaves, but when he comes back the brak is behind him. "They're turning the whole house upside down," he says. "Even Margaret's bedroom."

"I can't imagine what they're looking for," says my mother. "What do they think we're hiding in our home?"

If they find Benny's comics, my mother will be terribly angry. "No. They can't go into my hospital," I say. "Ward Three is down with Spanish flu and my Angela is terribly sick with bubonic plague. They mustn't come crying to me if they catch it."

My father gives the brak a skew smile. "It's just a child's game. You know, hospital-hospital?"

The man frowns, and all he says is: "There's a cupboard in the kitchen that's locked. Is there a key, or must we break it open?"

My father gives Gemima a nod. She puts down her embroidery, stands up and walks over to tell him.

"No whispering," says the brak. "Where's the key, hey?"

Gemima points: "It's up there on the shelf. In the vase."

Tomorrow she'll hide the Ann Wise cupboard key in a different place. But now I can see how Gemima's mind works. Very clever of her, but next time she won't fool me.

It's almost light, and I stretch out on the carpet with my head in Gemima's lap. I feel her cheek against mine, and there's the smell of Lifebuoy, her favourite soap. When I open my eyes again, it's daytime.

Gemima has gone, but her embroidery is still there, on the carpet.

A few days later, my mother says we're going to England. I tell her that holidays only start next month. I'll miss the last weeks of school, and I won't get to see the Christmas lights at Joubert Park or sing carols by candlelight.

She says she doesn't care, she's booked three tickets and we're leaving tomorrow night.

She's counted wrong. So I tell her, "You'll have to book another one because there are four of us."

My mother looks sideways and says, "You father won't be coming with us. He has to stay behind to keep the home fires burning."

I have to pack a suitcase of clothes, some summer ones too, even though it's going to be freezing in England and I won't be needing them. My mother says it's just in case.

"Please, Ellie, don't do this," says my father.

Gemima hasn't been at work for three days. The house is a mess and we've had to borrow the Desmonds' maid to do the ironing. She's not as nice as Gemima, but my mother says she'll have to do.

I ask my father when Gemima is coming home. He says he's doing everything he can, but things aren't looking too rosy, and so forth.

"But where is she?" I say.

"I'm still trying to find out, Mags. I promise, I'll make this better."

I believe him.

Lucy doesn't want to come to England with us. We've never been in an aeroplane before, and I tell her it'll be super-dooper. Lots of fun things, like the teeny bottle of Coca-Cola Benny's father got with his brandy when he flew to Canada, and the supper the air hostess brings on a special tray. I suppose Lucy's worried about Roger the Dodger, who won't have anyone to wash his clothes and take him food. But my father tells her she has to go, it's not debatable.

"You've read about what happens in detention," he says. "Solitary confinement breaks people. I know Gemima loves you, but it's only a matter of time before she cracks. You have to go. Please, Lucy, at least you'll be safe there."

"I can't, Daddy. Please don't force me to leave. I won't just run away and remain silent about it all."

"I forbid you to go anywhere near the security police. I absolutely forbid it. It's far too dangerous." His voice gets quiet. "Leave it with me. I've been making enquiries, and I'll go round to The Grays again first thing tomorrow. If they won't tell me where she's being held, I'll go to Marshall Square."

"You *must* speak to them. Please. Mima had nothing to do with what Roger and me were doing. She didn't even know what was in those boxes. I can't let her take the blame."

They stop arguing when I peep from under the kitchen table. They both look upset, so I don't ask whether Gemima's having a special holiday like Roger. She's always telling me she wants some peace and quiet, but she'll soon be bored to tears in Marshall Square.

Lucy goes off crying in her bedroom. She stays there the whole day, and refuses to come out, even at supper. I've been crying a lot, too. President Kennedy has been assassinated in America and it's a terrible tragedy, he was so handsome. I saw the picture of Jackie on the front page of the *Sunday Times*. She looked so sad.

Our bags are packed. I'm only allowed to take a few toys, and I have to leave my books behind. My mother says they'll make the aeroplane too heavy. All my dolls are too sick to travel, so I pack my stamp album. Also my pink jewellery box with the dancing ballerina. I've tidied my cupboards, with strict instructions to my father that Gemima is not to interfere with my things while I'm away.

My father takes us to the airport. Lucy's face is like a lump of plaster of Paris. She doesn't let my father hug her. Nor does my mother. He hugs me, though. It's as if he thinks he won't see me for an awfully long time.

He walks away from us, and I run after him.

Last touch!

JENNA

Holly manages to find parking a block down from Pembroke Street, where Miss Leventhorpe has arranged an after-tears tea.

We walk up the road, and Clever waves at me. He's guarding the cars, no worries.

People are shouting and laughing as they spill out of buses and taxis. A group forms a circle and toyi-toyis in the middle of the road. They stamp their feet and sing.

"Who are all these people?" I ask.

Holly shrugs. "From her political days. It's a good turnout, she'd have been chuffed."

Under the jacaranda tree on the front lawn there are two trestle tables with lots of fizzy drinks. Young people in ANC T-shirts are sprawled out on the grass. Some are talking, others are softly singing.

The smell of cooking reaches us as we walk in the front door. Two shiny-faced women push past us in the passage, one carrying a pot of steaming chicken and the other some pap. They're greeted with cheers from the garden.

The dining-room table is set with urns and trays of sandwiches. Holly and I help ourselves to a cup of tea and join some older people drifting along the passage with plates of food. The passage walls have discoloured patches where the pictures have been removed. Boxes line the sides.

Miss Leventhorpe has been busy finishing up the packing. There's no box marked for Holly, of course – I guess it was just Aunt C-C's way of trying to get her to come and visit.

As we loiter in the passage, I notice a man, grey-haired and wearing a dark suit. He's leaning against the wall, and from behind the cover of *Time* magazine, he flicks his eyes over the faces passing by. He's not reading, of course. He's watching for someone. I catch his eye and wink.

There's a clanging sound as a short, fat man marches out of the kitchen. He bangs a spoon against a pot and calls out, "Gather round, gather round!" At the front door, he yells at the laughing, singing crowd in the garden: "Speech time, comrades. Come, squeeze in if you can."

We follow him down the passage. The lounge has been emptied of furniture, with the carpet rolled to the side. The sash windows are open, and faces peer inside. People shuffle in until there's no standing room left.

"I would like to say a few words about our departed comrade," the man says. He pauses. "Those of you in the passageway, keep it down please, and maybe you'll be able to hear me."

An old woman waves her teacup in the air. "Comrade Harry, do we have anything to make a proper toast?"

He reaches into his satchel and produces a bottle of vodka. "Russia's finest. Share it around, comrades."

A group of old folk drain their cups and pour themselves a bit of vodka. The bottle comes our way, and Holly shakes her head. "Not for us, thanks. We're staying with the tea." I catch Miss Leventhorpe's eye as she pours herself a generous tot.

"To Comrade Lucy!" There's a general cheer as they drain their cups. "Hamba kahle, Mkhonto! We all knew and loved Comrade Lucy Channing-Court. We will never forget her tireless work for the movement in Britain, and the role she played in setting up the Truth and Reconciliation Commission in 1994."

Comrade Harry pulls out another bottle. "You didn't actually think there would be only one?" The crowd laughs, and the second bottle is passed around. Stretching his neck, he grins as he catches the eye of someone at the back of the room. "Comrade Nzuzo, it's good to see you've brought a bottle, too." The cups clink as they're charged again.

"Let us all raise our cups one last time to Comrade Lucy. Fiercely loyal, compassionate and honourable. Our comrade, our friend, a defender of the oppressed, a fighter for freedom! To Comrade Lucy."

Voices break into song as the cups are raised. "Arise ye workers from your slumbers. Arise ye prisoners of want …" From the garden, more voices join the swell. They eventually fade, and people disperse into the garden, into the kitchen, blocking the front door as they stop and chat. Holly and I make our way to the dining room where we get another cup of tea.

In front of me, a posh voice says: "Don't you dare hog all the sandwiches, Scumbucket. I'm watching you."

"Mags?" Dropping his magazine, the man opens his arms to the woman and drawls, "Hey, it's really you. How long has it been? Fifty years?" He lets her go, holds her at arm's length as he looks at her. "Well, I'll be damned! You haven't changed one bit."

"Fibber. I'm a granny now, coming apart at the seams." She throws her head back and laughs. "Must say, you've held up rather well." Her blonde hair is cut short in a no-nonsense style, and she looks trim in a navy-blue suit. The eyes behind thick glasses glitter. Anything but granny-ish.

"Just look at you," she says. "A successful Canadian banker, I've heard. I always knew you'd make money, Benny. You were such a clever-clogs at sums." With a chuckle, she punches his arm.

They carry on like this, firing words at each other like two kids at a paintball range. I fetch myself a biscuit, and when I come back they're still at it. "You're so lucky to have been here for the bar mitzvah. It was hideous being held up at Heathrow. I missed the funeral – and the speeches too, dammit," the woman says.

"Well, the bar mitzvah is actually next month. When I heard about Lucy's passing, I thought I'd come early and …" He breaks off and looks up at the ceiling. Then he glances down again, a shy smile on his face. "You see, I *knew* you'd come home for this."

It's obvious that these two oldies were close to Aunt C-C. I sidle up, my back to them, and listen hard. She guffaws, and I turn to look at her. The corners of her eyes have lines like sunrays. She's done a lot of laughing in her life. He holds out some kind of coin to her. "See, I kept it, Mags. All these years."

"Oh, put that away, Scumbucket," she says and laughs again. "The tea is on the house. And if you wanted to bribe me, you'd better know that I only take hundred-dollar bills." She picks up a plate and holds it out to him. "Another one of these?"

He puts the coin back into his wallet, helps himself to two sandwiches. "You stopped writing, Mags."

"Rubbish, you did." She shrugs, flashes a smile at him. "Well, maybe it *was* me. But I'm not conceding, mind. Possibly when I went off to boarding school in England. The penguins there were far worse than at St Vergilius. There was no time for mischief. Or for writing letters – apart from the obligatory Sunday-night ones to our parents."

Hey, she's talking about Virgins, calling the nuns penguins. She sounds *just* like Aunt C-C. I edge closer.

"I heard about your parents. I'm sorry about the divorce."

"Oh, Mummy couldn't conceive of a divorce, the Pope would have excommunicated her. They just separated and went their own ways. Poor Daddy was awfully lonely all by himself down here." She takes a sandwich off his plate, wrinkles her nose at it, and puts it down again whispering, "Botulism."

"Your father was good to my family. I'm sorry I didn't see him again."

"Daddy made two trips to see Lucy and me, but he spent most of the time in the pubs. It was awful, you wouldn't have recognised him. He died the day after Mandela was released. I was glad he lived to see that, at least." She tilts her head and says, "It was quite a moment, wasn't it, when the old man appeared on television. I never kept up with all the goings on down here, but even I was quite moved by it all."

This snooty-sounding woman is Aunt C-C's sister, I realise. The other girl in the photo on our passage wall, the one with the sly smile. As they talk, I search for a resemblance. It's the stubborn jaw, I decide.

"And your mother?"

"Oh, she didn't make it past fifty. The doctors said it looked like a stroke, but I think anxiety finally got her." She leans forward and takes his arm. "Why don't we slip away, and we can catch up properly? I don't recognise a soul here, other than you."

Please don't leave, I want to say. I never really got to know Aunt C-C, and here's her sister. I turn to the woman and blurt, "Excuse me, I'm Jenna Moore. I think we may be related."

"Jenny? My goodness, Lucy's second name was Jennifer. I wonder if you were named after her? What a pretty thing you are. Are you also a Channing-Court?"

"It's actually Jenna. And that's my mom over there, Holly," I say, pointing. She's chatting to a hot-looking guy with dreads as she twirls her hair with a flirty smile. Ag, Holly! She catches my eye and flutters her lashes at me.

I turn away and say, "You had an uncle called Frank, I think? Well, she's his granddaughter. So I suppose that makes me some kind of niece of yours."

"Extraordinary. Did you hear that, Benny? I have nieces I've never even heard of before. When we moved to England, Mummy had very little to do with the Channing-Court side of the family." Her hand grabs mine. "I'm Margaret Channing-Court, Lucy's younger sister." She turns to the man and says, "And this is a dear old friend of mine, Benny Schaumbacher. Would you believe, he grew up next door when I lived in this very same house."

Miss Leventhorpe appears in the doorway with another tray of sandwiches. She puts it on a table and comes up to me. "Jenna, may I interrupt? I'd like to introduce Margaret to someone. She's in the lounge, and has asked to meet her."

Margaret Channing-Court takes my hand. "Come, Jenna, I'm not letting you out of my sight," she says. "I want to know everything about you." She gives her friend a pat on the arm. "Make yourself useful, Benny. Go and chat to Jenna's mum. She's over there," she says with a sideways nod of her head. "We can all get together for a delicious natter afterwards." He hesitates, but she waves him away. "Go on, that's her – the gorgeous young woman in the green dress."

The lounge has emptied, with just a woman standing at the window, looking out over the garden. Miss Leventhorpe takes us over to her and says, "Judge Thabisa Ndlovu, may I introduce Doctor Margaret Channing-Court, Lucy's sister from London. And this is Lucy's great-niece, Jenna Moore."

"Thank you, Mary." The judge's eyes light up and I smile at her. "Jenna and I have already met," she says, a sympathetic look on her face. Miss Leventhorpe turns to leave, and the judge takes the doctor's hand. "I am so sorry for your loss, too, though I'm pleased to make your acquaintance. Your sister told me a lot about you."

"Your surname is Ndlovu, did I hear that correctly?" The doctor has a puzzled look on her face. Then, very softly, in a sing-song voice she says, "N-dlovu. N-dlovu, I love you, I love you." Narrowing her eyes, she looks at the judge. "You know, I once had a nanny with the same surname. Her name was Mavis ... no, Mavis was Benny's. Mine was Gemima. A relation of yours, by any chance?"

There's a silence as we wait for her reply.

"The woman you call Gemima was my grandmother. She had one child – my mother."

"Mm, I don't recall Gemima having a daughter. At least, she never mentioned one to me." The doctor smiles, and there's a glimmer of the little girl in the photo. "Gemima was perfectly marvellous. Lucy and I absolutely adored her." She turns to me and says, "You know, Jenna, when we went off to England, I missed her like mad. I wrote to her, I'm sure I did. But I don't think she ever wrote back. Even though she was literate."

"Your sister told me you were close to my grandmother. That she was like a mother to you. That's why I wanted to meet you." Picking up her briefcase, the judge says, "But I have to leave now. I'm expected in my chambers." Again, she holds out her hand.

"It's been *so* good to meet you," says the doctor, cupping the hand in both her own. "I can't imagine that Gemima is still alive, but I always wondered what happened to her. I know my father didn't need a full-time maid after we left for England. Lucy may have known, but she never told me. And then, well, I suppose I forgot about home. I do wonder, though: did Gemima go back to the farm?"

The judge closes her eyes briefly, and swallows. "No, she passed many years ago."

The story Aunt C-C told us at the hospital swirls in my head, together with bits I'd found on the internet about Gemima. The stuff about being born on my great-grandfather's sugar farm after the first world war, and working for the Channing-Courts for twenty years. The Rivonia trial and all, the police raiding the Pembroke Street house, finding incriminating material, being detained for nearly four months – and the *torture*, and her not breaking even though she knew who the boxes belonged to.

Gemima suffered all this to protect her beloved Lucy. After her release, sick with pneumonia, she'd called her employer, walking to a tickey box around the corner from the police station. From there, Doctor C-C took her to Pembroke Street, to Lucy's bedroom, where he tended to her. But this time, he could not make her better.

A voice cuts into my thoughts: "Fana? I'm leaving now. Be ready for me outside the gate." The judge slips her phone into her bag, and disappears into the crowded passage.

The doctor and I are walking to the front room, when she

says, "You see, Lucy and I drifted apart when we went to England. I was at boarding school, then I studied medicine. We were always too busy –"

Bustling up to us, Miss Leventhorpe butts in: "Margaret, I just want to let you know that Lucy packed your things into some boxes. They're in the passageway, and have your name on them. If you need a hand, I'll get a couple of the young people to help you with them."

But the doctor's attention has been caught by Mr Schaumbacher, who is still talking to Holly. I follow as she strolls over to where they're standing, and says, "Benny, let's drag these lovely people away and go somewhere nice. Perhaps we can have a spot of lunch later on?"

Holly smiles at me, and shakes her head. "I'm sorry, Jenna has a job she's due at in ten minutes, and then we have an appointment at the school. If you give me your number, we can always make a plan for another time?"

The doctor fishes in her bag and hands my mother her card. "Do ring me, I'll be here for at least a fortnight." She spins around and says, "Well then, it's just you and me, Scumbucket. We can spend the day talking about all the jolly times we had in the good old days."

Mr Schaumbacher looks at her. The smile sits stiffly on his face, and he lightly fingers his upper lip. "Yes, Mags, we can do that."

We bump into Miss Leventhorpe on our way out, and thank her for all the trouble she went to with the funeral arrangements and the tea.

243

"Your aunt was ever so fond of you, Jenna. I told her I'd keep an eye on you, and I will. Good luck for this afternoon." She gives me a hug.

Awkward.

Holly and I drive off, and I wave at Clever. He's helping Mr Schaumbacher pack boxes into the boot of a car. A few blocks down, I get out at 37 Klip Street. Holly's bagged an offer on the house, and the Frams are packing up. They fly to Ireland at the end of the week. I'm helping with the last few boxes, just a couple of hours' work.

"See you later," Holly says with a wave. "And don't forget to give Mrs Fram the spare set of keys."

Dianne Fram buzzes me in, "Thank God you're here," she says as she opens the front door. "Come this way, I'm busy in the bedroom."

I follow her down the familiar passage into James's room and get busy packing. Two hours and eight boxes later, Mrs Fram passes me a bubble-wrapped ornament and I settle it in a cardboard box, making sure that it fits snugly with the other pieces. Aunt C-C would have approved. I slip Katy's hockey badge into the box. I don't need it any more.

"I hate leaving," Mrs Fram says. "This is my home, my life. I can't stand the thought of Ireland. Imagine spending the rest of your life never seeing the sky."

Dianne Fram is as lovely as I'd imagined, but the stress of waiting for the house to be sold seems to have left its mark. Her voice sounds strained, and her eyes look tired.

"I mean, just think about it. Next week's forecast is five degrees in Dublin. And that's the *daytime* temperature." Biting off a piece of tape, she winds it around a bubble-wrapped vase. Her fingers get caught in the tape and she swears under her breath. "I'm going to *die* without the sun."

I take the tape from her. "So, why you going then?"

"Bobby says we just don't have a choice, we can't stay. Jamie still has terrible nightmares, the last home invasion was the worst for him. We had him in therapy for weeks, but it didn't seem to help. It's horrible, I feel so helpless."

Turning around, she calls out, "Robert, did you buy more tape? We're running on empty in here." She pauses as she waits for a response. Her mouth tightens. "I *told* him he should buy at least ten rolls of the stuff – should have got it myself."

Robert. She's angry with him. But it's not about the tape, of course.

"And Katy won't leave the flat; she sees danger everywhere. We just want to go somewhere where the kids can be safe. Even if it rains all the time."

I wish with all my heart that I could fold myself into Mrs Fram's suitcase and escape to Ireland with them. I look up at her and say, "I don't have a choice, I can't leave. I have to stay."

"I know there are thousands of people who want to leave, but can't. We're so lucky, Bobby got this job, and we can just go. But I feel so ashamed. It's like we're running away."

"You want your children to be safe. That's what parents

do," I say, then I start packing James's books. He'll want them in his new bedroom in Dublin.

"I just feel so betrayed." She turns to me, tears welling up in her tired eyes. "What the hell happened, hey? We were supposed to be the rainbow nation, and it's all gone rotten. I don't feel I belong here any more, I don't feel welcome in my own country. Twenty years ago, it all felt so different."

"I've got a friend," I tell her as I pick up Roald Dahl's *The Enormous Crocodile*. "Her name's Xoliswa, she says everything's all messed up because we lied about the past. Whites had the chance to come clean about the damage we did, but it was too hard for us. We thought we'd get away with pretending that nothing terrible ever happened. Just go on with life as normal. Except, it was never normal."

She grabs the book from me and shoves it in the box. "Well, I never hurt anyone. I never lied. I've always tried to be a good person. God knows, I never supported apartheid. I've got nothing to apologise for." Her cheeks are flushed. "Your Xoliswa should take responsibility for that government her people keep electing. *They're* the problem, not us."

Sitting on my haunches, I look her in the eye. "I don't think it's a question of them and us. We're all in this together. I don't really understand it all, and it's way more complicated than what Xoliswa says." I stand up, lightly touch her shoulder, and she flinches. "All I know is that we're angry," I go on. "All of us. We feel cheated. Everything's horrible and wrong, and now we're all terrified it can't ever come right. Everyone's blaming everyone else. It's easier that way."

She's still as a stone, her eyes staring like a blind person. She's about to say something when her husband pokes his head into the room. "I *did* buy more tape. I left it where I said I would, on the dining-room table." He walks around the room, inspecting. "Good, we're nearly finished in here. But the kitchen's still full of stuff."

"I thought you said you'd handle the kitchen?" She looks at her watch. "It's time for Jenna to go, and I have to pick Jamie up from school."

I pick up my bag from James's bed. "I'm sorry I can't stay to help with the rest. My mom will be waiting outside. I've got a meeting at the school, and I can't be late."

The gate clicks shut behind me and I cross the road to where Holly is waiting next to the car.

"You okay, baby?" She puts an arm around me. "You're doing the right thing. Aunt C-C would be proud of you. *I'm* proud of you."

I'm not okay. In about fifteen minutes I'll be in the principal's office. Holly and me on one side of a table. And opposite us, the principal, the legal advisor, and the chairman of the school board. I told Holly I didn't want a lawyer. I've thought about things a lot, and I know what I'm going to do. *If* I can hold it together. No – I *must* hold it together.

I'll stand up in front of them all. I'll tell them there was no silly misunderstanding between Andile and me. The truth is, there was nothing between us. Nothing at all. I, Jenna Moore, am a stupid, selfish liar. As damning as they look, the fact is, the photos lied.

I'll ask to meet with Andile. To apologise. Not alone, no. It's unlikely we'll ever again be alone together. He'll never again smile and look at me like he thinks I'm funny or brilliant. Not ever again. I really messed up. But I'll look him in the eye – I'll try, anyway. And try to find words to say how I've wronged him. I'll ask him to forgive me. And I won't blame him if he doesn't. I'm so scared and ashamed. But I'm not running away.

Yes, I'm going to do this. I *will* do this. I must. But I feel cold with panic. It'd be so much easier to say nothing. I could just leave, go to another school. Leave the whole ugly mess behind me. I could just do that.

Holly curses. "Oh crap, not again." She's crouched down on the pavement, scrabbling through her bag, trying to find the car keys. She catches my eye and swipes the hair away from her face. "Ag, sorry, baby. I'm so useless. Just give me a minute."

A minute. She can have all the minutes she wants from me. As many minutes as it takes to get to the moon and back. As many minutes as there are stars in the sky, and twice more than the planets in the universe.

"No problem, Mom, we've got time."

"Aha!" she says, dangling the keys from her hand.

And I remember: the keys. "Hey, hold on a minute, I forgot something." I walk across the road, drop the spare keys into the Frams' postbox, and give it a tap.

Last touch.

ACKNOWLEDGEMENTS

Many people helped me write this book. I am especially indebted to Gillian Godsell, Gill Murdoch and Penny Smith for sharing their childhood memories of Johannesburg in 1963. Thank you for being so patient with my interminable questions over the years. You allowed me to borrow your memories and I hope I have honoured them. I would also like to thank John Berks and Adrian Steed for their lovely recollections of Springbok Radio. And to Stephanie Kemp for allowing me to read her unpublished memoir, *My Life* – which has since been published, and Jeremy Clark – whose memoir, *Neroli*, I hope will one day be published.

Several people also made helpful suggestions during the various stages of the manuscript: Máire Fisher, Joanne Macgregor, Helen Moffett, Wynter Murdoch, Paige Nick, Emily, Sophie and Jack Robertson. Thank you for catching me.

My thanks to Andrew Unsworth and Keith Kirsten for their advice on all things gardening. Bottles of whiskey are riding on their insistence that loquats did indeed grow in Johannesburg in the autumn of 1963.

Bishop Forrester would like to thank Jane-Anne Hobbs,

Jenny Hobbs and Michael Olivier for cooking a supper fit for the pope, and for the delightful advice on table etiquette. (Sorry about the jelly in the trifle.) On matters isiXhosa, thanks to Charles Siboto, Mkhuseli Jack and Nolubabalo Tyam. In the end, I decided on the more modern forms of address. And thank you to Babalwa Shota for her advice on isiZulu usage. On matters Catholic, my thanks go to Chris Deeks and Carmel Rickard for setting this lapsed Anglican straight on the mysteries of the Catholic Church.

And to the helpful staff at the National Library of South Africa in Cape Town: thank you for hauling the newspapers out of the stacks and for setting up the microfiche machine, again and again. I have drawn from 1961–1963 news reports, headlines and captions in the *Rand Daily Mail*, *The Star*, *Cape Argus*, *Sunday Times*, *Volksblad*, *Die Transvaler* and *Drum* Magazine.

I am grateful for the assistance I received from Sahm Venter, Ronnie Kasrils and Sylvia Neame with regard to historical facts in 1963, and to Nicholas Wolpe and Ivornatte Chitambo for information relating to Liliesleaf. It is a marvellous heritage site, worthy of many visits. I have taken artistic licence, for example in the chapter on Liliesleaf, where I mention that the names of 173 witnesses for the prosecution at the Rivonia trial were displayed as an exhibit.

There were many other people who helped in the research and fact-checking for this book, including the teachers and learners at Sandringham High School. I am also grateful to Greg Arde, Ursula Bulbring, Martha Jane Evans, Mandy

Friedman, Sandra Hattingh, Steve Holland, Judy Klipin, Doreen Levin, Helen, Heather, Neo and Kabi McDonald-Robertson, Susan Russell, Shelley Seid, Elizabeth Sleith, Toni Strasburg, Kate Savage, and Facebook friends who tolerated my strange queries. And thanks, too, to JK Rowling for the levitating charm of *Harry Potter and the Philosopher's Stone*. Wingardium Leviosa!

Though I have tried to remain true to the events of 1963, I own any errors I may have made.

I have listed the books that I read while writing the manuscript. Hilda Bernsteins's memoir was particularly useful, and I drew from the descriptions of her daily trip to Pretoria during the Rivonia trial, as well events outside the Palace of Justice on 29 October 1963. Her accounts of the raids on her home in Observatory, Johannesburg, by the Security Branch were also extremely useful.

In conclusion, I would like to thank my publisher Michelle Cooper and all the staff at Tafelberg for the amazing work they do. And to my incredible editor Lynda Gilfillan, for her scalpel eye, her patience and humour, who spun gold out of the words I sent her.

And always, my love and thanks to Mike, Emily, Sophie and Jack, who feed me and put up with me.

www.edythbulbring.com

BIBLIOGRAPHY

Bernstein, Hilda. *The World That Was Ours*. London:
    Persephone Books, 2004
Carneson, Ruth. *girl on the edge*. Cape Town: Face2Face,
    2014
Frankel, Glenn. *Rivonia's Children*. Johannesburg: Jonathan
    Ball Publishers, 1999
Frankel, Hazel. *Counting Sleeping Beauties*. South Africa:
    Jacana, 2009
Gordon, Suzanne. *A Talent For Tomorrow*. Johannesburg:
    Ravan Press, 1985
Hirson, Denis. *I Remember King Kong (The Boxer)*.
    Johannesburg: Jacana, 2004
Joffe, Joel. *The Rivonia Story*. Bellville: Mayibuye Books-
    UWC, 1995
Kasrils, Ronnie. *Armed and Dangerous*. Oxford: Heinemann,
    1993
Lewin, Hugh. *Stones Against the Mirror: Friendship in the Time
    of the South African Struggle*. Cape Town: Umuzi, 2011
Mandela, Nelson. *Long Walk to Freedom*. Boston: Little
    Brown, 1994
Pinnock, Don. *They Fought for Freedom series: Ruth First*.

Pinelands: Maskew Miller Longman, 1995

Richards, Jo-Anne. *The Innocence of Roast Chicken*. London: Headline Book Publishing, 1996

Schermbrucker, Reviva. *Lucky Fish*. Bellevue: Jacana, 2003

Schneider, Anthony. *A Quiet Kind of Courage*. South Africa: Penguin, 2013

Slovo, Gillian. *Every Secret Thing*. London: Little Brown, 1996

Trapido, Barbara. *Frankie & Stankie*. London: Bloomsbury, 2003

Wolpe, AnnMarie. *The Long Way Home*. London: Virago Press, 1994

ALSO BY EDYTH BULBRING

The Summer of Toffie and Grummer

Cornelia Button and The Globe of Gamagion

The Club

Pops and The Nearly Dead

Melly, Mrs Ho and Me

Melly, Fatty and Me

The Mark

Snitch

Snitch2: A Year of Relative Madness

The Reject

www.ingramcontent.com/pod-product-compliance
Lightning Source LLC
Chambersburg PA
CBHW031714170626
46808CB00005B/1743

* 9 7 8 1 9 9 0 9 4 1 3 1 3 *